SLOW BURN DUET

Mychael Black

SLOW BURN DUET

Both Slow Burn books in one volume! Join Dr. Morgan Sears, his submissive Jamie Frost, Officer Austin Russell, and Austin's sub, Jared Haley, as all four men navigate new relationships, small-town life, and bigoted families. Through it all, they explore the world of BDSM and manage to fall in love.

This book is a work of fiction. Any resemblance to persons, living or dead, actual events, locale, or organizations is entirely coincidental.

Arian Derwydd Books, LLC

https://arianderwyddbooks.com/

Slow Burn Duet
Copyright © 2024 by Mychael Black

All Rights Are Reserved. No part of this book may be used or reproduced in any manner whatsoever without written permission.

FROST BURN

Being gay in rural Tennessee comes with all sorts of issues. For Jamie Frost, those issues stem from his bigoted father and brother. When he and his best friend go to Nashville for a bit of fun, however, Jamie meets a man who changes his life forever.

Morgan Sears swore he'd never return to his tiny hometown of Sawyer, Tennessee. Yet, return he has, determined to give the place the medical care its people need. He expects a bit of nostalgia, maybe even a bit of opposition. What he doesn't expect is to see the young man who managed to wrap himself around Morgan's heart after one night in Nashville.

Chapter One

If there was anything Jamie Frost hated more than this God-forsaken town, it was this damned suit. He scratched the back of his neck where the jacket collar rubbed him raw.

"James Thomas Frost," his mother admonished. "Quit fidgeting and, for God's sake, smile."

Fidgeting? Kids fidgeted.

"What sadist thought to make a suit out of wool?" he grumbled under his breath.

Mom turned him toward her, fussed with the collar a few minutes, and straightened his tie. "Hush now. You look good and 'bout as respectable as a man can be with long hair." She smiled up at him. "Your granddaddy's suit looks good on you. He wore this when your daddy and I got married."

That explained the mothball smell.

Jamie gave her his best smile and leaned down to kiss her cheek. "You seen Jared?"

"Think I saw him head outside to smoke. Take your jacket off if you go out there." Before Jamie could walk away, she caught his arm. "Thank you for comin' to your sister's graduation."

"You're welcome, Mama."

Jamie had the offending garment from Hell draped over his left forearm before he even made it out of the old high school gym. He ducked through the crowd congregated in the hall and reached the front door without anyone stopping him. He went outside and rounded the left corner of the gym. His best friend Jared was standing there, back against the red brick wall, taking one slow drag after another from a cigarette.

There *was* a God.

Jared grinned over at him and held out a pack, shaking it a little. Jamie took one, and Jared lit it, his own bouncing between his lips as he spoke.

"You look relieved."

Jamie inhaled and nodded, then blew the smoke out slowly. "I'm so sick of pictures. Mom's been taking them all day."

"Same here." Jared chuckled. He dropped his cigarette butt on the pavement and ground it out under the toe of his boot. "Renee is itching to leave town. What about Sheila?"

"Believe me, she's ready to hit the road. Hell, I can't wait to get the fuck out of here."

Jared nodded. "I get it." He glanced at Jamie. "Just a few more months. Then we'll have enough money to find a place somewhere else, far away from this close-minded shithole."

Jamie stared straight ahead and sighed. "Yeah." He finished his cigarette and put it out.

Jared laughed and draped an arm around Jamie's shoulders. "Come on. I have an idea."

They managed to get away from the school without anyone spotting them. As soon as they were out of sight, Jared stopped and turned him around.

"Let's go to Nashville for a few days."

"Seriously? Why?"

Jared shrugged. "No one will know us there, and I've seen some things online about where to find hook-ups. We can hang out and hit the bars, maybe find a couple guys who wanna have some fun."

Jamie blew out a breath and raked his hand through his hair. "All right. Just for a few days, though. Mama needs my help next week."

"Awesome. Let's pack a couple bags and get out of here for a few."

They headed toward their cars, and Jamie followed Jared to his place. Thankfully, everyone was at the high school, so they managed to get Jared's bag packed fairly quickly. The tricky part was getting Jamie's. His brother hadn't gone to their sister's graduation, which meant he and his friend Sam were probably getting drunk at home. As Jamie rolled up into the driveway, his fear was confirmed. Sighing, he shut off the car but didn't get out right away. A soft tap on the window drew his attention from the old trailer.

Nodding, he got out and shut the door.

"Want me to come inside with you?"

"No. If Daryl sees you, it'll only be worse. No sense in you dealing with his shit, too."

Jared shoved his hands into his pockets. "Okay. But if I hear anything I don't like, I'm coming in."

Jamie smiled at him. It felt good to have someone on his side. Then again, Jared had always been on his side. "Thanks. I'll be right back."

He could hear the football game blaring from the TV before he even opened the front door. With their backs to the door, he slipped down the hall. After ducking into his room, he packed as fast as possible. He grabbed the small cigar box where he'd been stashing his money and shoved it into the bag as well. Then he left his room. He almost made it to the front door.

"Where you goin', faggot?"

Jamie froze, his hand on the doorknob. He didn't bother looking at Daryl. "Just heading to Jared's for a couple days."

Daryl muttered something to Sam, and they both laughed. The sound was not pleasant by any stretch of the imagination.

"Fine. Go suck your boyfriend's dick, fag. I'll be sure to let everyone know."

Jamie walked out, slamming the door behind him. He no longer bothered to correct anyone whenever they insinuated -- or blatantly stated -- that he and Jared were a thing. They'd kissed one time, but they'd agreed it felt like kissing a brother. No thanks. Jamie got to his car and tossed his bag in through the open window.

"I'm ready. Please get me the fuck out of here."

"Understood. How about we leave my car at my uncle's and take yours?"

Jamie nodded and got into his own. "I don't know how much longer I can do this."

Jared leaned down, arms resting on the door frame. "Hey. I get it. Your situation is worse, I know, but you're not alone, Jamie."

"Thanks."

"Come on," Jared said, patting Jamie's shoulder. "Time to blow this joint for a few days."

* * *

Several hours later, they were sitting in one of Nashville's best gay bars, sipping beers and just enjoying being away from Sawyer for a while. Country music kept the dance floor full with all sorts of people and pairings. It felt like a different world.

Jared bumped his shoulder. "That dude's been watching you since we walked in." He discreetly tipped his bottle in the direction of a single man sitting at a table. The guy was indeed looking at them.

Jamie studied him for a moment. Not a cowboy, but just as ruggedly handsome. Definitely older, with near-black hair cut short, the slightest hint of gray at the temples. He was built, but not overly muscled. Those biceps hadn't come from a gym, but the man didn't seem to be the type to do hard labor either. He looked like a lawyer, to be honest. A hot, almost-silver-fox lawyer, dressed in a suit that somehow looked casual and not uptight.

Even from across the room, Jamie felt those dark eyes on him like a touch.

The sensation unnerved him, and he took another swig of beer. His nerves were all over the fucking place.

"You gonna go say hi?" Jared asked him.

Jamie wanted to. God, he wanted to. "I don't know. He's… intense."

Jared chuckled. "Okay, I won't argue with that. He looks like he wants to fucking devour you."

Jamie shivered. That's precisely what he'd thought. He took another drink to steel his nerves because he *really* wanted to go over there, but he didn't get a chance.

The silver fox was headed their way.

Up close, he was hotter than anyone Jamie had ever seen.

"A dance?"

Jamie nodded, utterly mute. He took the man's outstretched hand and stood. The man led the way to the dance floor, and a slower song began. Jamie found himself hip to hip, chest to chest, trapped by eyes almost as black as the man's hair.

"What's your name?"

"Jamie. Yours?"

"Morgan Sears."

Jamie watched those lips move and had never wanted to kiss someone so fucking much. Morgan's mouth beckoned him like a moth to a flame.

"Something on your mind?"

Morgan's voice slid through Jamie like a hot knife through butter. He couldn't stop the shiver that slithered through him. Morgan smirked, the expression sexy as sin yet arrogant as hell.

"I asked you a question, boy."

"Yes," Jamie whispered.

The hold around his waist tightened, and he had only a second to process anything before Morgan's mouth captured his own. Jamie had only kissed one person in his life. Experiment or no, not even Jared could've prepared him for such a soul-consuming kiss. Morgan's arm felt like steel where it wrapped around Jamie's waist, while the other hand slid through Jamie's hair and tugged. Jamie whimpered against the man's mouth, the spark of pain sweet and so fucking amazing.

"I'm staying in a hotel about a block away," Morgan murmured. "I want nothing more than to see you all spread out on my bed, naked, hard, and begging."

"Oh, my God." Jamie moaned and nodded. "Please."

"Go tell your friend you'll be at the Holiday Inn, room 112. Got a phone?"

"Yes."

"Get it so I can give you my cell number. He needs to have it, too."

"Okay."

Morgan released him, and Jamie headed back to the table. It was a miracle his legs even worked.

Jared smirked up at him. "That went well, I see."

Jamie's hand shook as he picked up his phone. "I'm… I'm going to his hotel room. Holiday Inn, 112. He wants to give me his number and said to make sure you have it, too."

"Oh, take-charge kind of guy," Jared said with a grin. "Nice."

Jamie could only nod and turned. Morgan stood right behind him. Jamie handed the man his phone without question. Morgan typed something into it, and the text notification pinged. He handed the phone back to Jamie.

"That's me," Morgan said. "Send your friend here a text so he has my number."

"Yes, sir," Jamie muttered. He shot off a text to Jared and looked up. Something in Morgan's expression had changed, and those eyes were darker, more intense, if that were possible. Jamie swallowed.

"Let's go," Morgan said. He took Jamie's hand, they both said goodbye to Jared, and headed out of the bar.

Chapter Two

"What the hell was I thinking?"

"Your guess is as good as mine. Not sure what the fuck a Daddy Dom is going to do in Sawyer, to be honest."

Morgan Sears stared out the front window of his new office and sighed. "Tell me about it. This place has changed so fucking much, and, yet, it hasn't changed at all."

Austin chuckled, and Morgan thought he heard the man's desk chair creak. One of these days, that damn chair was going to give way and dump Austin's smug ass onto the floor. "I'd ask if that's even possible, but Sawyer is stuck in the past. That's why you're there, to help get the town into the twenty-first century, medically at least."

Morgan groaned and turned away from the window. There wasn't much out there anyway. His new practice sat along a side road near downtown, though he used the term loosely for this place. He and Austin had grown up here, but they'd been smart and got the hell out of Dodge the second they'd graduated high school. Now here he was, twenty-five years later, back home in an effort to drag his hometown kicking and screaming into the present.

He thought back to a few days ago, to an encounter he was sure he'd never forget. He'd gone to the bar in Nashville just for the hell of it, not even intending to hook up with anyone.

Then he'd met a stormy, thundercloud gray gaze from across the room.

Fuck, the boy had been absolutely perfect. So sweetly submissive, so eager to fucking please. Morgan had taken that beautiful ass many times that night, and he still heard Jamie's moans and whimpers and pleas in his head days after the fact.

"Earth to Morgan."

"Sorry. Just zoned out. I need to go into town. The printer should have my order ready."

"I'll be there in a few days," Austin said. "The transfer should be finalized by then. Just gotta tie up some loose ends here."

"You're gonna have your work cut out for you," Morgan said. "Lots of crime, you know."

"Fuck you," Austin said with a laugh.

"Yeah, we tried that once, remember?"

Austin snorted. "Some Doms may be able to pull that off, but we would've killed each other."

Morgan wasn't going to argue that point. They'd had sex one time years ago, but they were both just too fucking dominant and controlling to handle one another. Nope, best friends was where they belonged.

"Anyway, I need to get going myself," Austin said. "Will touch base tomorrow, man."

"Sounds good."

Morgan hung up and looked around the front lobby. He had no idea what the building had once been, but it was starting to resemble a clinic finally. There were three exam rooms, his private office, two restrooms, the lobby, and, of course, a tiny lab for running quick tests. It would work for now.

He grabbed his keys, turned off the lights, and headed out to his car. When he'd rolled into town last night, he'd been too damn tired to do anything but crash in the hotel bed. Just a few more days, and he could sleep in his own. The house remodel was almost done.

First stop was the town's only print shop where he hoped his order waited. Flyers, business cards, door decals, pamphlets. He was determined to get this place up to speed in terms of medical care. The townspeople shouldn't have to drive nearly a damn hour to Sevierville just to see a doctor.

As he drove along what amounted to downtown's 'main street,' he took stock of the buildings. Most were, surprisingly, in use, though they still looked rather rundown. He pulled up outside one storefront a few doors down from the printer and just stared.

"Holy shit."

Frost's General Store had been around for ages. As teens, he and Austin had hung out here with Harlan and Mitchell Frost. Their grandfather had started the store long, long ago. Morgan couldn't believe it was still in business. A couple of rocking chairs sat out front, and an old checkerboard sat between them on a wooden barrel.

Morgan got out and just shook his head. "Wow."

The bell over the door jingled when he walked inside. It felt like he'd stepped back in time.

Although the store seemed to carry a lot of modern products, not much had changed in the overall appearance. There were still broken tiles on the floor, faded wooden shelves, battered tin signs hanging on the walls.

"Can I help you?" a man from behind the counter asked.

Morgan didn't recognize him, but that wasn't really surprising. "Just looking around, to be honest." Morgan approached him, hand outstretched. The man shook it, nice and easy, though maybe a touch wary. "I'm Morgan Sears."

The man's eyes widened. "The new doc?"

"That's me," Morgan said with a nod. "I haven't been home in quite a long time."

"Kurt Haley," the man said. "Nice to meet you." He waved around the store. "We've been trying to get Harlan to update this place, but he's a stubborn ass."

Morgan snorted. "He always was." At Kurt's curious expression, he continued, "I grew up with Harlan and his brother. There were four of us, actually. Austin Russell will be here in a few days to take over at the station."

"I'd heard we were gettin' a new police chief. He's gonna have his hands full with the Frost boys, that's for sure."

"Frost boys? Harlan's?"

"Yep. Only one is a Frost, but he and his friends are trouble. I keep trying to get my nephew to leave 'em be, but Jared and Jaime, Harlan's youngest, have been friends since they were in diapers."

"Trouble how?" Morgan asked, hip cocked against the counter, arms crossed. He'd told Austin he'd scout out any potential issues.

"Rowdy, few bouts of vandalism, drinkin', that sort of thing. I think a couple of the boys have light fingers." Kurt shrugged. "Not to mention rumors runnin' rampant about Jamie. Another reason I want Jared to step back."

"What kinds of rumors?"

Kurt leaned close, voice lowering. "Folks say Jamie Frost is one of them 'boys,' if you catch my meanin'."

One eyebrow rose as Morgan studied the man. He was tempted to play ignorant and make the man actually say the word, but he didn't. "I see. Well, I'll be sure to keep an eye out for any mischief then."

Kurt nodded. "Best of luck to you there. Jamie's got a temper on him."

Morgan resisted the urge to roll his eyes. "Thanks for the heads up. I gotta hit the print shop, but I'll be around. Good to meet you, Kurt."

"Likewise. Take care, Doc."

Morgan pulled his cell out of his pocket and hit number one on the favorites list.

"That was quick," Austin said.

"I think one of Harlan's boys is gay."

Whatever Austin had been drinking was most likely now all over the man's desk. He spluttered and coughed before regaining his wits. "What?"

Morgan started down the sidewalk toward the print shop. "Remember their general store? I got to talking with the clerk there, Kurt Haley, and he told

15

me some juicy Frost gossip. Apparently, Harlan's youngest son and his friend are the bad boys of the town, and rumor has it that Harlan's kid is queer."

"Damn," Austin muttered. "I can't begin to imagine Harlan liking that."

"Same here. Kurt said they'd most likely be the ones to keep an eye on. Minor vandalism, rowdiness, minor theft. That sort of thing. Far cry from Houston, but probably enough to keep you from getting bored."

"No shit."

"Anyway, just wanted to share that tidbit of interesting news," Morgan said. "No doubt I'll run into Harlan or his brother at some point."

"I'm so not looking forward to that," Austin grumbled.

"Neither am I. They were bad enough in high school. God forbid they find out we both like dick, too."

Chapter Three

They'd been home for nearly a week, but Jamie hadn't gone back to the trailer. Instead, he'd crashed in the tiny apartment over the garage at Jared's folks' place. They weren't fond of him, but they also knew his own home life was less than pleasant. He rolled over and stared up at the ceiling.

He couldn't get Morgan out of his head. He'd tried, telling himself over and over that it had been a hook-up and nothing more. Which it had been. Hell, the man had been staying at a hotel, so clearly not from the area. Jamie wondered where Morgan was from, where he was headed. Did he even remember the night they'd spent together?

Jamie figured this was what went through a chick's mind when she lost her virginity. He hadn't told Morgan that tidbit for fear of coming across as an inexperienced kid -- even though he kinda had been.

Sighing, he rubbed his face with his hands and grabbed his cell off the floor by the bed. Ten in the morning. He really didn't want to get up, and he sure as fuck didn't want to go back home. Mama needed his help, though, and aside from Jared, she was the only one in the family who really understood him. She had no idea he liked men, but he had the feeling she'd accept him if she did.

He got up and stretched. Hell, he still ached, as if Morgan's heavy-handed touches lingered all over his body. Christ, that man had gotten under his skin somehow, and Jamie wasn't sure how to feel about it.

Shoving those thoughts away, Jamie dressed and left the loft apartment, locking the door behind him. Then he went downstairs and climbed into his car. Jared was most likely at work, serving assholes at Carl's Diner. Jamie had tried that job, but he didn't react well to being told what to do. His temper had gotten him fired within a couple of days. Jared was a fucking saint to put up with that shit. Then again, he was a saint for putting up with *Jamie's* shit.

The drive home didn't take long, and Jamie parked in his usual spot off to the side. At least Daryl's truck was gone. Jamie got out and went inside.

"Mama?"

"In the mudroom," she called out.

Jamie went back there and just shook his head. He helped her down the ladder she had no business being on. "What on Earth are you doing?"

Mama swiped a hand over her forehead, pushing back a loose bit of hair from her face. "I asked your brother to do this last night, but he fell asleep."

"You mean he drank his stupid ass into a stupor."

"Now don't be startin' on him. He's under a lot of stress."

Jamie wanted to argue about Daryl's 'stress.' The asshole had knocked up his girlfriend, and now they were scrambling to sort shit out. "Yes, Mama."

"Good boy." She smiled and patted Jamie's cheek. "You've always been my sweet baby boy."

Jamie wanted nothing more than to confess everything in that moment, but he bit his tongue. It wasn't only Daryl. Their father was just as bad. What Mama saw in him, Jamie had no fucking idea.

"Anyway, what did you need help with today?"

"I gotta run some things downtown. Oh, and I've got an appointment with that new doc who just came into town. Beats driving all the way to Sevierville."

"Agreed. Well, let's load stuff up into my car, and we'll head that way then."

They managed to fit all the things she wanted to donate to the Goodwill into his car, and then they set off. He'd heard about the doc coming, but he hadn't done any research. Not that he would've needed to. Aside from the occasional fight, most with Daryl or Sam, he was fit and healthy.

They dropped off her donations, and then they walked down the street to Carl's Diner. Within a few minutes, they were seated in Jared's section.

"Hey," Jared said with a smile as he approached their table. "Usual?"

Mama beamed him a genuine smile. She was the only one in the family who actually liked him. "Yes, sweetie, thank you."

"Sounds good," Jamie told him.

Jared left to get their drinks -- Coke for Jamie, sweet tea for Mama. Mama unfolded her napkin-wrapped silverware and placed her napkin in her lap. She seemed to fuss over it, which meant she had something on her mind.

"Mama."

She sighed and looked up at him. "I love you. You know that, don't you?"

"Of course. I love you, too."

"I will always love you, no matter what."

Jamie swallowed, and his world narrowed. The din from the rest of the diner faded.

Mama reached over and put her wrinkled hand on his, giving it a gentle squeeze. "It's okay, baby."

Remembering how to breathe, he stared down at their hands. "How...?"

"A mama just knows," she said. "I know you can't tell your daddy or brother. Hell, I probably wouldn't say anything to your sisters. They gossip worse than church ladies."

Jamie chuckled and felt something loosen around his heart. He glanced up at her. "Thank you, Mama. I... I love you so much. I was so afraid to tell you."

"I know, but you will always have my support, no matter what your daddy or brother have to say."

Jared returned with their drinks. As he set them down, he seemed to sense the mood between them. Jamie smiled up at him and mouthed, 'later.' With a nod, Jared left to tend to another table.

"So, this new doctor," Mama said before taking a sip of her tea. "You know he went to school with your daddy? There were four of them who hung out, I think. Your daddy, your uncle, Morgan Sears, and Austin Russell. I think Austin is going to be our new police chief, too."

Everything went absolutely numb.

Jamie didn't hear a single word beyond 'Morgan Sears.'

"Jamie?" Mama asked. "You okay, baby? You look like you've seen a ghost."

Shaking his head, Jamie struggled to plaster on a normal, I'm-perfectly-fine face when he felt like the wind had been knocked clear out of him. "I'm okay."

Mama eyed him for a moment before launching into stories of the antics his father, uncle, Morgan, and Austin had once gotten up to as teens. When Jared delivered their food, he raised an eyebrow at Jamie.

"Mama, I'll be right back. Restroom."

Jamie slid out of the booth and, gesturing for Jared, headed toward the hallway where the restrooms were. As soon as they were out of sight, Jamie slumped against the wall.

"Oh, fuck." He scrubbed his hands down his face, feeling physically ill. "Fuck, fuck, fuck."

"Dude. What's wrong?" Jared rested a hand on his shoulder. "Jamie?"

Jamie stared straight ahead, brain going in a million directions. "The guy in Nashville. His name was Morgan Sears."

"Okay..."

Jamie met Jared's gaze. "Our new town doctor is Morgan Sears. He grew up here."

Jared's eyes widened. "Holy shit."

"Jared... I lost my fucking virginity to a man old enough to be my dad -- who *knows* my dad."

"Okay. We can handle this," Jared said, as level-headed as always. "Right now, you're gonna go wash your face. Calm down. What happened earlier with your mama?"

"She knows I'm gay," Jamie said. "She's okay with it."

"So at least there's some good news," Jared said. "Go on. Wash up and go eat. We'll get through this." He pulled Jamie into a tight hug. "I promise."

Chapter Four

Morgan leaned back in his desk chair and closed his eyes for a moment. He'd been out of sorts since the Nashville trip. The kid -- well, maybe not a kid, Jamie had to be at least twenty-one -- hadn't left his mind. The way the word 'sir' sounded on Jamie's tongue had set Morgan's pulse racing like nothing ever had before. He hadn't even deleted Jamie's number from his phone. He'd thought about texting a few times, but then he'd gotten swept up in preparations for today. He'd already seen two patients this morning, and his next one was due at any moment. Sighing, he got up and straightened his tie and coat.

Half an hour later, the sweet lady was ready to leave. She'd been thrilled to have a doctor in town finally. He didn't remember her, but he sure recalled her husband.

"I'm sure Harlan would be happy to meet you for a drink," Aida said as they walked toward the waiting room.

Morgan chuckled. He couldn't imagine having anything in common with that man any longer. "Aida, I --"

He froze.

Sitting in one of the chairs, looking just as dumbstruck as he felt, was the last person Morgan expected to see.

"You haven't met our son," Aida continued, completely oblivious. "Jamie, this is Dr. Morgan Sears. Dr. Sears, this is our youngest, Jamie."

As Jamie stood, Morgan forced himself to remain absolutely still. Hand extended, Jamie's gaze never wavered. There was strength and utter steel in those eyes, which now resembled a brewing storm.

"Nice to meet you, Jamie," Morgan said. He shook Jamie's hand, holding on just a little longer than necessary.

"Likewise," Jamie muttered.

Morgan released him with more reluctance than he cared to admit. "Well, Aida," he said, turning to Jamie's smiling mother. "It was a pleasure to meet you and your son. I need to get back to it, but Harlan is welcome to call me."

It was a lie, really. Harlan Frost had been a prejudiced asshole back then, and Morgan couldn't imagine that would've changed. He also wasn't going to bring it up in front of the man's incredibly sweet wife -- or Jamie.

As they walked out, Jamie gave him a curious, wary glance. Morgan put just enough heat into his own to let Jamie know he hadn't forgotten Nashville.

Oh, no. He remembered every fucking detail.

"Teresa," he said to the receptionist, "when is my next patient?"

"Four o'clock, Dr. Sears."

"Good. I'm going to take an hour for lunch. You do the same, okay?"

"Thank you, Doctor." Smiling, she locked the computer and grabbed her purse from under the desk. He'd lucked out when he found her. "Are you going to lock up for lunch, or do you need me to?"

"I can. Take an hour and enjoy."

She headed out, and Morgan locked the door behind her, flipping the Open sign to Closed. He adjusted the little clock sign to indicate when they'd be back. Then he turned and went to his office. His appetite had fled, but he needed to eat. He grabbed his keys, draped his coat over the back of his chair, and left the clinic.

Carl's Diner was only a short walk away, so he didn't bother with the car. As soon as he was seated, he opened the menu.

"Hi, welcome to Carl's. My name is… Oh, shit."

Amused, Morgan glanced up, but his words died on his tongue. Jamie's friend stared at him like a deer in headlights. "Small world."

"Sorry," the man said, head shaking. "Sorry. I'm… Jared. I'll be your server. Um, can I get you started with a drink?"

"Ice water and a Caesar salad are fine," Morgan said. Before Jared could leave, Morgan continued, "I saw him already. Just thought you might want a heads-up."

Jared didn't say anything for a moment, but then seemed to gather his thoughts. He glanced around, then leaned closer, voice lowering. "He hasn't stopped talking about you. Just so you know."

"Likewise."

Straightening back up, Jared smiled. "Good. We can chat in a few, if you'd like. I'll be off in about twenty minutes. Let me get your drink and salad."

Morgan watched him walk away and sighed. What the fuck was he going to do? He hadn't been able to stop thinking about Jamie, but he also hadn't ever expected to see him again. And if Jamie was Harlan's son, then he most definitely was not out.

A few minutes later, Jared returned. He set everything down, then surprised Morgan by sliding into the booth opposite him. "I just clocked out. Look, just so you know, Jamie isn't out. Hell, he just now told his mother. I'm the only one who's known the rumors were true. Well, some of them. Some idiots think we are together, but we're not. He's my best friend."

Morgan nodded and started on his salad. "I grew up with his father and uncle. I'd hate to know what sort of shit Harlan would say or do if he knew."

"Jamie's brother, Daryl, is just like Harlan, though more vocal and nasty about it." Jared studied Morgan for a few minutes before continuing. "Jamie, well, he…" He sighed. "You were his first."

Morgan raised one eyebrow. "Coming from Sawyer, I can't say I'm too surprised. I do think he needs to be careful, though. Not every guy is going to be nice. Jamie wears his heart on his sleeve, and that can come back to bite him in the ass."

Jared tilted his head, staring at Morgan with a curious expression. "You're the first person to ever see that. I mean, yeah, Jamie has a temper and lets it get the best of him sometimes, but, deep down, he's sweet and kind."

Morgan finished eating and pushed the bowl away. He sat back and sipped his water, contemplating how much to say. Then he figured he'd just lay it out there. "I'm not usually the type to go cruising. I prefer a different sort of lifestyle."

"I know," Jared said. Morgan blinked at him, and Jared laughed. "We may live in Sawyer, but we *do* have Internet here. Jamie has never expressed any interest in that sort of thing, but I've done a lot of research. He knows what a Daddy is."

"It's more than that. *I'm* more than that."

Jared nodded. "He told me you were controlling, like *really* controlling."

"I'd like to see him again. I know he has to be careful, and I completely agree with that." Morgan pulled out a business card and flipped it over. Then he wrote his address and cell phone number on the back. "The ball is in his court now. Give him that. If he wants to know more, and possibly explore this, tell him to call or text me."

"I will." Jared looked up as Morgan stood. "I think he needs it, to be honest. He's a mess."

Morgan pulled out two twenties for his lunch check, took Jared's hand, and curled the young man's fingers around the money. "I agree. I'll talk to you later, Jared. Thank you."

The second he stepped outside, Morgan pulled out his phone and hit number one.

"Lunchtime?" Austin said by way of greeting.

"Remember that gorgeous, naturally submissive boy I had while in Nashville?"

"Yeah…"

Morgan stopped walking and closed his eyes as he stood on the sidewalk. "Austin… he's Harlan's youngest son."

"Holy fuck," Austin muttered. "Uh… I mean…"

"Precisely my reaction when I walked Aida Frost out to the lobby earlier today and met her 'baby boy.'"

"What are you going to do?" Austin asked.

"I want to see him again," Morgan admitted. "There was a spark that night, something undeniable between us."

"Does he know what you are?"

"No, but his best friend Jared does now. Jared is a server at the diner where I just had lunch. We got to talking, mostly about Jamie. I gave Jared my card and asked him to give it to Jamie. We'll see where it goes."

Austin blew out a breath. "Hopefully, it won't blow up in anyone's face."

"Agreed. When will you be rolling into town?"

"Tonight around nine. You still cool with me crashing at your place for a few days until mine is ready?"

"Of course. Will see you then."

"Sounds good. Gotta hit the road in a few. See you later."

Morgan hung up and continued toward the clinic, mind going immediately back to that night in Nashville…

* * *

"Strip, boy. I want to look at you."

Morgan sat in the armchair and watched as the lean body before him was slowly revealed. Smooth, pale skin came into view as each piece of clothing dropped to the floor. Stormy gray eyes held his gaze, and shoulder-length dark blond hair framed a boy-next-door face. Morgan couldn't wait to feel those sweet, full lips wrapped around his cock.

"Come here."

Jamie approached him, body beginning to shake just the slightest bit. Anticipation? Nervousness? Perhaps both.

Morgan gripped the boy's hand and tugged. Jamie tumbled onto Morgan's lap sideways. Morgan shifted him so Jamie's legs draped over the arm of the chair. Then he slipped his own hand between Jamie's muscled thighs, moving higher. Jamie sucked in a breath, bottom lip caught in his teeth.

"Open your legs, boy."

Jamie did as instructed, and Morgan cupped those sweet balls. Jamie moaned softly, hips rocking upward. Morgan chuckled and let his fingertip dip lower to brush over the tight puckered hole.

"Please…"

"Such a sweet boy," Morgan purred. "Begging me for more."

He moved his hand up and circled the base of Jamie's hard, slender cock with his fingers. Jamie's head fell back, and his entire body trembled. Morgan bent and sucked up a mark on the pale flesh of Jamie's neck, earning himself a sultry, needy groan.

"Bed," he said, releasing Jamie altogether. "There's lube on the table. Put on a show for me."

Jamie got up and went to the bed. Lube in hand, he lay back and spread his legs wide. Two slick fingers sank into that tight ass, and Jamie's moan slithered through Morgan.

"That's it," Morgan said as he approached the bed, undoing his pants. He let them fall to the floor, and Jamie's gaze zeroed in on Morgan's thick cock. Morgan unbuttoned his dress shirt and tossed it onto the other bed. "Are you ready for me, boy? Is that tight hole nice and slick and needy?"

Jamie licked his lips, breath speeding up as Morgan settled between his legs. "Y-yes, sir."

Morgan groaned and captured that wicked mouth with his own. Jamie's entire body rose up to meet him, brushing their cocks together. Morgan got the rubber on, then drew Jamie's still-slick fingers from the boy's hole to Morgan's cock. They slid along Morgan's length, stroking, teasing.

Morgan gripped Jamie's wrist and pinned it on the bed above the boy's head. He did the same to the other one, holding both in his left hand as he lined up his cock with his right. Then he thrust into the hottest, tightest fucking ass he'd ever had. Jamie arched beneath him, crying out and bucking to drive Morgan deeper.

"Please!"

Morgan took him hard and fast, Jamie's arms pinned in place, cock grazing Morgan's abs with every thrust. Morgan kissed and bit Jamie's throat and shoulder, drinking in the pleas, the cries of pleasure.

"Come, boy," he whispered, voice gruff as he held onto his own. "Come on my cock."

Jamie nearly sobbed out his release, semen spilling between their bodies. Morgan growled and kissed him hard, several fast strokes pushing him over the edge as well. Jamie whimpered, that lean body writhing and milking every last drop from Morgan's cock.

Morgan finally eased his hold and pulled Jamie's arms down. He massaged the strained muscles, kissed his wrists. Jamie's soft sounds surrounded them, as if he just couldn't get enough of Morgan's touches.

By the time the sun rose, Morgan knew he would never have another boy in his arms like this one.

Chapter Five

Jamie stared at the card Jared handed to him. *Morgan Sears, M.D.*

He leaned back against the tree, his thoughts a chaotic mess. He hadn't expected to see the man again. Ever. Yet there Morgan had been, in the same casual slacks, dress shirt, and tie he'd worn in Nashville, all topped by a white doctor's coat with his name embroidered on the left breast pocket. Hands that had turned Jamie's world upside down in one amazing night had led Jamie's mother into the waiting room and shook Jamie's hand like they'd only just met.

"He wants to see you again."

Jamie closed his eyes. "There's more, isn't there?" When Jared didn't answer right away, Jamie chuckled. "So what is he? Just a Dom?"

"Well… not exactly," Jared said. "Remember when we were reading about the Daddy/boy stuff?"

"Yeah."

"Morgan's a Daddy Dom. It's a mix of the caregiver thing and the innate need to dominate and be in total control."

Jamie thought back to that night and how Morgan had given him various orders, how he'd had sat in Morgan's lap, Morgan touching him, how the man had held him down to the bed and blown his fucking mind.

"I get it," Jamie said. "I just don't know how to be submissive or a… boy. I hate people telling me what to do."

31

Jared snickered. "Believe me, I know. But you did with him, didn't you?"

"Maybe? I mean, he wasn't mean or nasty about anything. He didn't demand I do this or that. He just..." Jamie shrugged. "... told me do something, and I did it without question. It was weird -- and so fucking *hot*."

"I think maybe you could give it a try," Jared said.

"But don't Doms -- and Daddies, for that matter -- have rules? Not sure how well that will fly."

"From what we've read, Daddies, even Daddy Doms, have rules to help their boys, not just to control them. What did that one site say? 'Daddy knows best.'"

"Would he want me to call him that?" Jamie wondered aloud.

"What did you call him that night?"

"I never called him Morgan. I think I said 'Sir' a couple times, but that's because he's older. Kinda ingrained in me to call an older man that, you know."

"True. How did he react when you did?"

Jamie would never forget the flash of pure fire in those dark eyes. "I'm pretty damn sure he liked it."

"So call him that," Jared said. "Use 'Sir' unless he tells you to call him something else."

Jamie sighed. "I'm not gonna lie. A part of me is fucking terrified. Not of him, but of what he is."

"I get that," Jared said. "Honestly, I'm a bit more worried about your family. He knows your dad."

"Yeah, that's the other issue. I mean, he's gay, so I highly doubt he kept in touch with Dad all these years."

"That said, I think it's worth exploring," Jared said. "I wish I was in your place, to be honest. I'm a bit jealous."

Jamie reached out and put his arm around Jared's shoulders, tugging his friend close for a side hug. "You'll find your man. I don't doubt that at all."

"I hope so," Jared said with a sigh. "Someone tall, strong, wearing a uniform."

Jamie chuckled. "You and your uniform fetish."

Jared shrugged. "What can I say? I like what I like."

A twig snapped nearby, and they both froze. This was *their* place, the one spot where no one bothered them. Situated in the woods, but still visible from the road, this was where they came when they needed to talk without anyone hearing a word.

A figure emerged, and they both stood.

"We aren't trespassing," Jared said before the person came into view.

A cop. Fuck.

Jamie squared his shoulders and stepped slightly in front of Jared, who was a few inches shorter and a bit leaner. "We don't want any trouble."

The man stepped into the fading sunlight shining down from a break in the trees. Jared grabbed Jamie's arm and squeezed.

"Relax, boys." The cop smiled at them. "Name's Officer Austin Russell."

"Holy shit," Jared whispered from behind Jamie. "He's... hot."

"Morgan's friend?" Jamie asked, ignoring Jared for a moment.

"That's right." Officer Russell looked around the area, then back at Jamie and Jared. "Everything okay out here?"

"Why wouldn't it be?" Jamie asked him.

"Got a few calls about a black bear wandering close to a couple homes. Just wanted to check it out." He tilted his head, as if trying to peer around Jamie. "You okay?"

Jared stepped out a little. "Yeah." His hand trembled where he still had hold of Jamie's arm.

Officer Russell smiled. "Good to know. Look, I'm not gonna run you two off, just be safe out here. I'd hate to explain to Morgan should something happen to you, Jamie. As for you..." he said, looking at Jared. "Well... you come find me if you ever need anything."

With that, he tipped his hat and left. Neither of them said a word until they were sure he was out of earshot.

"Oh, my God."

Jamie turned, giving his friend a smirk. "I'm not carrying your ass back to the car if you faint."

"Did you see him?" Jared asked, completely ignoring Jamie's incredulous look. "He was... holy shit..."

Rolling his eyes, Jamie grabbed Jared's shoulder and pointed in the direction of where they'd parked his car. "Go. You can drool over the nice officer later."

* * *

Morgan glanced up from the pile of paperwork sitting on the desk in his home office. "How was your first shift?"

Austin grinned and dropped into the armchair near the desk. "Quiet aside from a few calls about a black bear too close to homes. And, apparently, too close to a couple cute boys."

The way he said it caught Morgan's attention.

"They okay?"

"Oh, yeah. Your boy's protective of his sweet friend."

"Pretty sure it's mutual." Morgan sat back in his chair, arms crossed. "Kills me they're all each other has. Jamie's mother seems to be okay, but the rest of their families, especially the Frosts..." He shook his head. "I can't say I'm too surprised."

"Yeah. I ran into Jared's uncle earlier, I think. Kurt. He doesn't seem too bad, but I've not met any other Haleys. Haven't ran into any Frosts either."

"Give it time. I'm sure one of us will encounter Harlan or Mitchell at some point. Not that I'm looking forward to it." Morgan stood and headed for the kitchen. Austin followed him. "Hungry? I haven't done a lot of shopping yet, so I thought we'd go to the diner. Good food."

"Sure." Austin leaned against the door frame, hands shoved into his uniform pants. "Those boys are..." He shook his head. "I don't know. I don't like them being anywhere near Harlan or Mitchell."

35

"Or Daryl," Morgan said. "Harlan's oldest. According to Jared, he's just as bad as Harlan, if not worse."

"Kurt warned me about the Frost brothers, but I'm really starting to think Jamie isn't the issue here."

"You're probably right. You change, and then we'll head over to the diner."

"Sounds good."

Austin went into the guest room while Morgan grabbed his keys from where they hung beside the front door. He studied the other spare on the ring. Austin had one already. Morgan was still pondering the idea when Austin returned in jeans and a T-shirt. He took one look at Morgan's keyring and chuckled.

"Has he even talked to you about pursing this thing between you two?"

"Not yet." Morgan pocketed his keys. "You drive."

They left the house and headed for the diner. About fifteen minutes later, they were sitting in a booth, perusing the menus. The server brought their waters, took their food orders, and disappeared again. Morgan had his glass almost to his lips when he noticed Austin's gaze lock onto the front door. Morgan twisted and cursed under his breath, setting down his glass. Harlan Frost hadn't changed in twenty-five fucking years.

"Well, hello, boys!" Harlan said in a boisterous voice loud enough to wake the dead. As it was, nearly every head in the diner turned toward them. "Morgan Sears and Austin Russell. I'll be damned." Harlan grabbed a chair, spun it around, and straddled it at the end of their table.

"Hello, Harlan," Austin said. "How've you been?"

"Oh, good, good. How's it feel to be home?" Harlan asked them both.

"Like we stepped through a fucking wormhole," Morgan grumbled.

Harlan's laugh was like fingernails down a chalkboard. Morgan met Austin's gaze and saw the same pained expression. The server brought their food, and Harlan made a show of flirting with her. She couldn't be older than Jamie or Jared.

"How's Aida?" Morgan asked pointedly.

Harlan waved off the question. "Eh, good. She's at church, doing God knows what."

"What about your kids?" Austin asked before taking a bite of his meatloaf. The question seemed innocent enough, but Morgan knew the intention behind it.

Harlan's expression was one of pride. "Daryl's a good boy, a chip off the ol' block."

"And Jamie?" Austin asked.

That pride turned ugly, morphing into disgust that made Morgan's stomach twist into knots. "Damn boy is a menace, lemme tell ya." Harlan leaned closer, voice dripping with venom. "Folks sayin' he's a fag." He sneered, and Morgan wanted to punch the bastard.

Austin's grip on his fork was murderous. "Not something to be sayin' in polite company, Harlan."

Harlan huffed and sat back. "Boy's worthless."

Morgan set his fork down, appetite completely gone. "Excuse me."

He headed to the restroom, needing to get away from the bastard before he killed him. He stepped up to the sink and splashed cold water on his face. The door opened behind him.

"He left," Austin said. "Something about needing to get back home."

Morgan met Austin's gaze in the mirror. "I need to get Jamie out of that fucking house, Austin."

Austin sighed. "I know, but unless his life is in danger, my hands are tied, Morgan. Besides, he's a grown man. He can leave anytime."

"Then I'm going to give him that option. The last thing we need is for you to arrest me for killing his father."

Chapter Six

"Dr. Sears?"

"Yes, Teresa?"

"Um… you have a walk-in. Your next scheduled appointment isn't for another hour. Can you see him?"

"Of course. Put him in room two, please."

"Thank you, Doctor."

Morgan got up and headed to the room. He grabbed the chart out of the door holder and knocked on the door. Then he opened it just as he read the name on the chart. His head jerked up, and he saw red. He shut the door, tossed the chart on the counter, and went straight to Jamie.

"What in God's name happened?" he asked as he turned Jamie's battered and bruised face first one way and then the other. There were cuts in several places, one eye well on its way to becoming black, abrasions, bruises. It took every ounce of willpower he possessed not to drag Jamie home.

"My brother," Jamie muttered.

Morgan's jaw tightened. "Tell me what happened." He left 'boy' unsaid, but from the look in Jamie's gray eyes, it was loud and clear. He grabbed supplies to clean the worst cuts and started on them, keeping his touches as gentle as possible.

Jamie shrugged, then winced. Morgan finished cleaning him and began unbuttoning Jamie's shirt as his boy told him everything.

"Daryl started up with his usual shit, calling me fag, cocksucker, sissy. You name it, he probably said it.

39

I finally got tired of listening to him run his mouth. I hit him. Next thing I knew, he had me on the floor, hitting, screaming, kicking."

Morgan gently slipped the shirt off of Jamie's shoulders, and his breakfast threatened to make a reappearance. Bruises and very obvious boot prints covered Jamie's torso.

"Down," Morgan said, easing Jamie back onto the table. "Anywhere else?"

"No," Jamie whispered. He closed his eyes, but not before Morgan spotted wetness in them.

"I've got you, boy," Morgan murmured. He ran his fingers over the bruises. "I need to get some X-rays to make sure nothing is broken. Don't move."

Jamie nodded, and Morgan stepped out of the room.

"Teresa, I need the portable X-ray, please, and call Officer Russell."

"Yes, Doctor."

Morgan took over with the machine and finished rolling it into the room. He got it set up and took several pictures of Jamie's torso from various angles. Then he pushed the machine back out of the room. When he returned, Jamie was still sitting up, hands braced on the exam table's edge, head hanging down.

"Jamie." Morgan stepped closer and ran his fingers along Jamie's cheek. "You can't stay there."

"I have no place to go. Jared's folks aren't fond of me."

Morgan took his keys out of his pocket and removed the spare house key. "Now you do."

Jamie's gaze narrowed, but he took the key. "I can't --"

"You can," Morgan said, "and you *will*."

Fire flashed in those eyes, defiance warring with need and desperation.

"You can argue all you want, but you know I'm right."

Before Jamie could answer, there was a knock on the exam room door.

"Come in, Austin."

Jamie cursed under his breath when Austin stepped into the room.

"Good afternoon, gentleman," Austin said, all business. "Jamie? Mind telling me what happened?"

For the next few minutes, Jamie told Austin what Daryl had done. Austin took notes, nodding. When Jamie finished, Austin looked from Jamie to Morgan.

"I can take him in for assault and battery." Austin glanced back at Jamie before continuing. "That said, I don't think going back to your place is wise."

Jamie opened his hand to show Austin the spare key.

"Good." Austin gently patted Jamie's shoulder. "I'll be in touch. Doc, may I see you in the hall please?"

Morgan followed Austin out into the hall and shut the door.

"This is going to be nasty. You know that, right?"

"I know," Morgan said. "And I don't give a damn. Austin, Daryl could easily have killed him."

Austin took off his hat and raked a hand through his hair. "I know, I know. I need to get over to the Frost place. I'll let you know how it goes. He give you any trouble about staying with you?"

"Not yet. I think he's still in shock, to be honest."

"All right. I have no idea when I'll be there tonight. Just… promise me you'll lock all the doors and windows and don't let anyone inside except me." He seemed to think about something, then added, "see if maybe Jamie can convince Jared to go over there, too."

"I'll try."

Morgan watched him leave, then went back into the room. Jamie was slipping on his shirt, and Morgan helped him. Then Morgan began buttoning it up.

"I'm not fucking helpless."

"I know you're not," Morgan answered. He kept buttoning. "Do you think you can talk Jared into coming over, too?"

"Why?"

Morgan stepped back before he gave into the urge to pull Jamie into his arms. "Austin's worried your dad may stir up shit with Jared once Daryl's in custody. My house is fully outfitted with a security system, and, until his place is done with remodels, Austin is staying there. It's safe."

Jamie let his head fall back, and Morgan spotted another mark. It looked like someone had held him by the throat. Unable to stop himself, Morgan reached out and traced it with his finger, his hand shaking.

"The only marks on your body should come from me."

Jamie caught Morgan's hand and brought it to those sweet lips. Jamie kissed Morgan's fingertips. "Agreed. Sir."

Morgan curled his fingers around Jamie's. "We need to talk tonight. About a lot of things."

The rest of the day seemed to drag by after Jamie left. As promised, he texted Morgan to let him know he'd gotten into the house okay. Morgan finished up with his last patient and wasted no time gathering his things. By the time he got home, his nerves were all over the fucking place. He sat in the car in his garage, eyes closed, just trying to calm himself. A soft tap on the window came a few minutes later.

Morgan got out and pulled Jamie into his arms right then and there. He pressed a kiss to Jamie's hair and just breathed in the scent of whatever shampoo Jamie used. Jamie's arms snaked around Morgan's waist, fingers fisted in Morgan's sportscoat.

"X-rays were okay," Morgan said without letting go. "Nothing's broken, thank God." He gently tipped Jamie's head back to see his face. "Your eye is gonna look rough for a bit." He traced a finger along Jamie's lower lip. Then he gave in and retraced the path with his tongue.

Jamie opened for him without hesitation, and Morgan dove into the kiss, putting all his desire into it. Jamie's hold on his coat eased, but then those hands slipped Morgan's shirt out of his slacks and pushed right up under it to glide over Morgan's bare skin.

"Inside, boy," Morgan said. "Let's eat and talk. Is Jared coming?"

"He is. He's also absolutely pissed."

"Good. I'd be worried if he wasn't." Morgan pulled back and shut the car door. "To the kitchen."

Chapter Seven

"Sit."

As he sat on one of the barstools, Jamie watched Morgan take out stuff to cook. With the man's back to him, he admired the muscled body that had rocked his world just a few weeks ago in Nashville. Morgan was everything Jamie had ever dreamed of, even if the man was a bit controlling. Okay, maybe more than a bit.

"Can I ask you something?"

"Of course," Morgan said as he set a pot of water on the stove.

Jamie had no idea what he was cooking, but it had to be better than the ham sandwiches Jamie usually had for dinner. "Are you a Daddy Dom?"

Morgan turned and leaned on the bar across from Jamie, his dark eyes warm yet penetrating. "I am."

Jamie hadn't expected that answer. He'd expected Morgan to deny it or maybe even get defensive. Most people did when Jamie's filter failed to kick in. Instead, Morgan just smiled.

"Oh."

"My turn," Morgan said, and Jamie nodded. "What do you know about it?"

Jamie shrugged. "Only basic stuff, like rules, terminology, that sort of thing. From what Jared and I have read, every situation is different. In all honesty, I don't know how to be a… boy. Or a sub, for that matter."

Morgan turned back to the stove to add pasta to the pan. "I'm happy to know you've read up on it. You're right about every relationship being different. No two Daddies or boys are alike. Even more so when adding a D/s dynamic into the equation." He glanced over his shoulder at Jamie. "As for you not knowing how to be a boy or a sub, rest assured: you very much are."

Jamie thought on that while Morgan gave the spaghetti a stir. In another, shallower pan, Morgan crumbled up hamburger meat and got it started. Then he washed his hands and returned to the bar.

"How?" Jamie asked him.

"In Nashville, I wasn't looking for that. Hell, I don't think I was really looking for anything, to be honest," Morgan said. "Then I saw you. I saw the need, the hesitant defiance in your eyes. I knew I had to get my hands on you, even if for just one night. You were perfect for me, Jamie. You still are. I don't want soft, unquestioning compliance. I want a challenge. I want a boy who keeps me on my toes but who also knows what it means to turn everything over to me. I demand submission, and I promise to always have your back no matter what."

Jamie swallowed as he stared into those gorgeous eyes. Could he seriously give up all control to someone else? The idea terrified him as much as it turned him on. He had to look somewhere else just to think clearly. "What about rules?" he asked as he stared down at the bar's marbled surface.

"One rule is eye contact," Morgan said, slipping a finger beneath Jamie's chin to tilt his head back up. "Always."

"Yes, Sir," Jamie murmured.

Morgan smiled. "Good boy. Now, before we get too much into this discussion, there is a very important thing to discuss: safe words. I imagine, given the research you and Jared have done, that you know what it is."

Jamie nodded. "We both do, Sir."

"The easiest to remember is the stoplight sequence. Red for full-stop, no questions asked. Yellow is to slow down. Green means all is well and to keep going. Safe words apply to *every* situation, from sex to conversations. Understood?"

"Yes, Sir."

"Good. Now back to the rules." Morgan opened a drawer in the bar and pulled out a piece of paper. He slid it over to Jamie. "I wrote them out last night. They're rules I've always had, but I added a few new ones tailored to our current situation. You read them, and I'll answer any questions."

Jamie took the paper, and Morgan went back to cooking dinner.

1) Honesty on both our parts, no matter how difficult the truth may be. Communication is paramount to a healthy relationship.

2) Begin every morning with a text if we are apart or a kiss if we are together.

3) End every night the same way: text or a kiss.

4) Daddy is always in control. Specific situations will be dealt with as they arise, but in the bedroom, there is no exception to this rule.

5) Daddy must know where you are at all times. This is to make sure Daddy can get to you if you need help.

6) Daddy will help with establishing a healthy diet and lifestyle, including exercise, regular check-ups, and mental health. This includes smoking cessation.

7) When in the privacy of home, you will dress in a way that appeals to Daddy.

8) You will always be ready for Daddy, inside and out.

9) If you have any concerns, you will talk to Daddy and not hold them in.

10) In return, Daddy will always care for you. He will make sure you're safe and healthy. He will always have your back in every situation.

"That's… a lot," Jamie said. "When you said 'in the bedroom,' what all does that mean?"

Morgan put the lid on the pan with the sauce and gave the spaghetti another stir before turning to face Jamie. He crooked his finger. Jamie slid off the stool and stepped around the bar. Morgan reached out and caught Jamie's jeans, tugging him close.

"It means *everything* that happens in the bedroom, be it vanilla or during a scene, is mine to control. When we are at home, you will be plugged at all times, aside from necessary bodily functions. During sex, you will wear a cockring until I am ready to release your cock. You will not touch yourself except to wash. Finally, and most importantly, you will *never* come without my permission."

Jamie shivered and pressed closer. Despite the voice in his head vehemently protesting giving up all that control, his cock practically ached it was so fucking hard. "Sir…"

Morgan smiled and kissed him softly, no tongue but just enough pressure to make Jamie want to beg for more. "Soon, I expect to hear something else from that mouth of yours, boy. Normally, I would have you strip for me, but since we won't be alone until bedtime, you may keep your jeans on. However…" He gripped the bottom of Jamie's shirt. "Arms up."

Jamie lifted his arms, and Morgan tugged his shirt off before handing it to him.

"Hamper is in the bedroom by the closet. Remove your shoes and socks, too. I like bare feet. When you are done, come back in here and sit. We have more to discuss before Austin and Jared arrive."

"Yes, Sir."

"Last door on the right down the hall."

Jamie headed down the hallway and opened the bedroom door. The décor screamed 'Morgan.' Dark wooden furniture, a huge bed, pale cream-colored walls and carpet. Everything seemed to have a place. Even the most fastidious neat freak would be envious. Jamie found the hamper and put his jeans in it. He tugged off his shoes, set them beside the hamper, and tossed his socks into the hamper as well.

Then he returned to the kitchen and took his seat at the bar again. Morgan was finishing up dinner and plating their spaghetti, topping it with sauce. He nodded toward the four-person dining table.

"Table, boy. We have water, milk, grape juice, Pepsi. What would you like?"

"Um, Pepsi, please," Jamie said. "Thank you, Sir."

Morgan placed the plates on the table. "We can talk while we eat." He returned to the kitchen area for silverware and their drinks, then sat down at the table. "Now that we have the rules set, I want to know more about what *you* want."

Chapter Eight

Morgan watched Jamie as they ate. His boy was nice and toned, but he had the feeling Jamie's diet wasn't the greatest. Easy enough to fix, though he anticipated a bit of resistance down the road when it came to the healthy lifestyle rule. One big sticking point he expected would be the smoking habit. He had no idea how long Jamie had been doing it, but it needed to stop. Morgan detested the smell, and the health impact was just too much.

"I do have one question," Jamie said before shoveling a bite of spaghetti into his mouth.

Morgan nodded and sipped his water. "I'll answer anything. I imagine, as time goes on, you'll have quite a few more as well."

Jamie took a drink of Pepsi and refocused on his plate. "About the smoking rule…"

"I will help you quit," Morgan said. "But, yes, it is a rule. I don't like the smell, and it's unhealthy."

"I started when I was seventeen. It's stress relief, honestly."

"There are other, far healthier ways to relieve your stress," Morgan pointed out. "We will explore your options. There are also many avenues for smoking cessation I can prescribe as well."

Jamie opened his mouth to reply, but Morgan held up a hand. He knew what Jamie was worried about, and this was the perfect opening for another potential hurdle.

"Caretaking is part of this," Morgan said. "That encompasses all aspects of your life, including finances. If you wish to work, that's perfectly fine. However, I will be paying for everything, including medical care."

Morgan finished eating and pushed his plate to the side. Jamie ate the last few bites of his dinner and set his fork down.

"That was amazing. Thank you."

"You are quite welcome. Did you have anything to ask about what I said?"

Jamie shrugged and cradled the Pepsi can between his hands, staring down at it. "I... I haven't been to a doc in a while, but that's mainly because I've always been pretty healthy. Well, aside from the smoking and occasional drinking. Our family doesn't really have much money, so whenever there is a bit extra, it usually goes to my mom's doctor bills. My dad refuses to step foot in a doctor's office."

"Yeah, I can't picture Harlan doing anything someone suggests, even if it's for his health."

Jamie snorted. "Would it be bad if I said I'm glad? I know it sounds horrible, but if he were to fall over dead tomorrow, I wouldn't mourn him."

The look in Jamie's eyes was tortured and angry. Morgan wanted to erase the pain, but he knew only time would heal such things. He held out a hand, and Jamie got up. As soon as Jamie was within reach, Morgan tugged him over until Jamie straddled his lap.

"It doesn't sound horrible, not after all the shit that bastard -- and your brother -- have put you through," Morgan said. It took considerable effort to keep the vitriol out of his voice. It was a damn good thing he swore an oath to heal people; otherwise, he'd gladly find a way to rid the world of Harlan and Daryl Frost.

"You're so not a typical doctor," Jamie said with a chuckle.

"I have a vested interest in seeing them face justice."

Jamie smiled, arms draping over Morgan's shoulders. "I've never met anyone like you."

"Likewise." Morgan gripped Jamie's hips and pressed their bodies closer together. Jamie moaned when Morgan's hardening cock flexed beneath him. "Now tell me what you want out of this. If you indeed want it."

"I do," Jamie said. "God, I do. I've always fantasized about finding someone who has my back, you know? I mean, Jared does, but that's different. I always wanted a lover who would know what I needed and when I needed it."

Morgan nodded and ground Jamie's ass down onto his lap as a reward. Jamie moaned and squirmed. "What sorts of things have you thought about doing?"

"You mean fantasies?" Jamie asked him, voice low and husky and breathless.

"Yes, boy. I want to know everything you think about when you're stroking that beautiful cock of yours."

Jamie groaned, eyes rolling. "Sir…" He gasped when Morgan brushed a hand over his erection. "I've only had my fingers before… before Nashville, but I always thought about it. When I jerked off, I'd think about having my ass fucked hard and fast, my hair pulled, my ass slapped. In my head, my lover would talk dirty to me, tell me how good I am, how much he loved my ass."

Morgan's cock pushed against his pants, more than ready to slide back into his boy's tight hole, over and over. He kept his hand resting over Jamie's straining erection and lifted the other to wrap in Jamie's long hair. Then he tugged -- hard.

"Sir!" Jamie's fingers dug into Morgan's shoulders, and the lean body shuddered from head to toe.

Morgan smiled and rubbed his hand over Jamie's denim-covered cock just a bit harder and faster. He tightened his grip in Jamie's hair. "Come for me, boy."

Shouting, Jamie jerked, hips bucking against Morgan's hand as his cock flexed and pulsed in the tight jeans. Morgan groaned and, using his hold on Jamie's hair, tugged Jamie down for a hard kiss.

"Oh, my God," Jamie panted against Morgan's mouth. His heart thundered so hard, Morgan felt it.

"Let's get you cleaned up. Go to the bedroom and undress. Then wait for me."

Nodding, Jamie stepped back a little. He looked at the table. "Do you need help?"

"Not tonight," Morgan said. "My sole focus is going to be you for the evening."

A car door shut outside, and then someone knocked on the front door.

"That's Jared," Jamie said.

"Go let him in. Then go to the bedroom. I'll get him settled in here."

"Yes, Sir." Jamie hesitated for the briefest moment before placing a chaste kiss on Morgan's lips.

Morgan cleared the table of their dishes and got out two more plates, silverware, and two glasses. He put them on the bar just as Jamie and Jared entered the kitchen.

"Wow. Your house is gorgeous," Jared said.

Morgan smiled. "Thank you. I've made spaghetti for dinner. Jamie and I already ate. Austin will be here soon as well. What would you like to drink?"

Jared watched Jamie head down the hallway before turning back to Morgan. "Pepsi?"

"Sure." He dished up some spaghetti and set it on the table. Then he handed Jared the silverware and his drink. "Jamie is waiting for me, so please excuse us. Make yourself at home, Jared."

"Thank you, sir."

"You're very welcome. We will be back out in a while."

Leaving Jared to his dinner, Morgan went to his bedroom. He found Jamie sitting on the bed, gloriously naked. Morgan gestured toward the master bathroom. With a curious expression, Jamie entered the large room as Morgan turned on the light.

"Oh, wow," Jamie said. "This is huge."

"I like having a good bit of room." Morgan turned on the shower and tested the temperature. Then he undressed and stepped into the spacious stall. "Come on, boy. Time to get nice and clean."

Jamie joined him, and Morgan pulled his boy close. Hands on Jamie's buttocks, Morgan maneuvered them until Jamie was under the warm spray. Jamie let out a moan that was part relaxation and part sex. Morgan's hard cock pressed between their bodies as he squeezed those gorgeous asscheeks in both hands.

"We'll start with your hair," he said as he reached for the shampoo. He got some in his hands and started working it through Jamie's long hair.

"Oh, God," Jamie groaned. "No wonder people goes to salons. That feels so amazing."

Morgan chuckled and continued running his fingers in Jamie's hair. "Rinse."

Jamie closed his eyes and tipped his head back, letting Morgan get the shampoo completely rinsed out. Morgan repeated the process with conditioner and loved the way Jamie practically melted against him.

"Time to wash the rest of you."

Morgan soaped up his hands with his bodywash and started at Jamie's broad shoulders. He massaged and rubbed, slowly and methodically washing every single inch of skin he touched. Jamie's gaze remained on his own, heated, needy. When Morgan reached Jamie's waist, he knelt and worked his way down to his boy's feet. Jamie held onto the bar on the side while Morgan washed each foot, keeping his touches firm enough to avoid tickling. Then he moved back up to Jamie's cock and balls.

Jamie sucked in a breath as Morgan cleaned him thoroughly. Morgan loved the soft whimpers Jamie fed him.

"Turn around, boy."

Swallowing thickly, Jamie turned.

"Reach back and open yourself," Morgan instructed. When Jamie did, Morgan rubbed the exposed puckered hole with his fingertip. He stood and reached up for the custom showerhead. He showed it to Jamie, not missing the gasp. "Inside and out, boy. It will fill you, and you'll hold it. I will give you privacy to finish up, and then you'll join me in bed."

"Oh, God…"

Morgan grabbed the bottle of lube he kept in the shower and slicked up the nozzle-shaped showerhead. Then he began pushing it into Jamie's ass. Jamie moaned and rocked back onto it.

"Hold it," Morgan instructed. He flicked the switch to divert a little bit of water into the nozzle.

"Oh, fuck," Jamie gasped, going up on his toes. "Sir…"

"Bend forward."

When Jamie did, Morgan turned up the amount of water. Jamie moaned and braced one hand on the shower wall while the other still gripped one asscheek. Morgan's cock dripped precome as he held the showerhead nozzle inside Jamie.

"Sir," Jamie said with a groan.

Morgan reached around and massaged Jamie's belly gently. "Just a little more, boy. Then you can finish up."

Half a minute later, Morgan shut off the water and slid the nozzle out. Jamie's hole clenched tight, and Morgan barely resisted the urge to tease his boy with a fingertip. Instead, he hung up the showerhead and stepped out of the stall.

"Give it about five minutes, then you can use the toilet. When you're done, give yourself a quick wash and join me."

Morgan watched Jamie shiver and smiled. Then he dried off and left the bathroom, giving Jamie privacy.

Chapter Nine

He hadn't stopped shaking. Not even the second, quick shower had eased his nerves. When Jamie stepped out into the bedroom, naked, he hadn't known what to expect. Instead of sitting or reclining on the bed, Morgan waited in an overstuffed chair, still dressed. The sleeves of his light gray dress shirt were rolled up, revealing his muscular biceps and forearms. The top button of the shirt had been undone. He hadn't even taken off his dress shoes.

"Come here, boy."

Jamie walked over, and Morgan gripped his hand. Just like he'd done in the hotel, Morgan pulled Jamie down onto his lap, draping Jamie's legs over the arm.

"Open your legs," Morgan instructed. When Jamie did, Morgan slid his hand up between them as he spoke. "This is our ritual. I'll clean you, inside and out, and then you will sit in my lap like this."

That hand inched its way higher, and Jamie bit his lip to keep from begging for more.

"Eyes on mine."

Jamie looked into Morgan's eyes, unable to escape the man's ungodly intense gaze. "Yes, Sir." He struggled not to close his eyes when Morgan's fingertips brushed his balls and just beneath them.

Morgan shifted him until he was reclining back into the man's right arm. "You will keep your legs open for me at all times when we are in this room." The words were punctuated by Morgan's fingertip pressing just barely into Jamie's hole. "There will be

59

things we do that may not make sense, but I feel they
are necessary. Spankings are not punishments. They
are a way for you to let go and just feel."

"Spankings?"

Morgan maneuvered him until Jamie was
draped over the man's legs, his chest on the chair's arm
and his ass bared. The first smack landed, startling
Jamie. He bit back any sound for fear that Jared would
hear him. Morgan slapped his ass again, this time a bit
harder. Jamie hissed and grabbed the arm of the chair.
The spanking continued, each blow stinging and
making every inch of Jamie's skin burn. Between each
one, Morgan rubbed his hand over Jamie's abused
flesh, and the heat and sting took Jamie's breath away.

By the time the spanking stopped, Jamie's head
swam, and his cock leaked steadily where it was
trapped between Morgan's thighs. All Jamie could
think about, all he could feel, was the burning warmth
of Morgan's hand on his sore asscheeks.

"Such a good boy," Morgan murmured. He
spread Jamie's cheeks, and two slick fingers stroked
over Jamie's hole. "If you come, there will be
punishment." He pushed his fingers inside, and Jamie
moaned.

Morgan's fingers twisted, turned, spread
Jamie's hole open over and over. Jamie dug his own
fingers into the chair's arm and couldn't help but push
backward. Morgan added a third finger and scissored
them.

"Sir," Jamie gasped. His thighs trembled, and
his hips jerked upward. "I can't…"

"You will," Morgan said. He withdrew his fingers, and Jamie wasn't sure if he wanted to protest or not. "On the bed, boy. On your back, legs up and open for me."

Despite his legs feeling like jelly, Jamie stood and went to the bed. He crawled onto it and turned over. Then he pulled his legs up and spread them open, holding them behind his knees. Morgan didn't move for a moment. He just sat there in the chair, his gaze raking over Jamie's exposed body like a touch. Finally, he got up, but he still didn't undress.

He picked up a cloth and wiped the lube from Jamie's hole. Before Jamie could ask anything, Morgan bent and nearly folded him over. Jamie couldn't stop the shout when Morgan's tongue pressed into his hole. He'd never felt anything like it.

"Sir!" Jamie shivered and struggled to keep hold of his legs. "Oh, my God. Please. I need…"

Morgan reached for something, and then a strip of leather wrapped around the base of Jamie's hard, aching cock.

"Oh, fuck," Jamie groaned.

Morgan returned to his previous position, face pressed against Jamie's ass as the man's tongue pushed inside again, over and over. Jamie moaned and panted, entire body beginning to shake. His cock throbbed, and he dug his fingers into the backs of his knees.

Finally, Morgan rose up. Jamie met those dark eyes as Morgan freed his own cock. Morgan took his time sheathing and slicking himself, and every stroke of his hand up and down that beautiful cock made Jamie's hole clench in anticipation. Then Morgan grabbed Jamie's hips and tugged him closer. Morgan's cock slid right on in like it fucking belonged there.

"Fuck, boy," Morgan grunted as he began thrusting hard and fast. His fingers dug into Jamie's hips, jerking him into every stroke. "Love your hole wrapped around my cock."

Jamie couldn't look away from those eyes. When Morgan nailed his gland, Jamie cried out, no longer giving a damn if anyone heard him. Then the cockring was gone.

"Come, boy," Morgan growled, slamming into him. "Come on Daddy's fucking cock."

"Yes!" Jamie bucked, entire body shaking apart as come spurted up onto his stomach.

Morgan groaned and ground against him. Jamie felt the man's thick cock pulsing deep in his ass and wished to God there was nothing between them. Morgan slowly eased out of him, got rid of the rubber, and wiped them both with the cloth. Then he dropped down onto the bed and tugged Jamie into his arms.

Just like Nashville, Jamie had no idea what to say. Words had escaped him, and his mind was a weird mix of nothing and yet everything. Morgan seemed to sense it as well.

"Shh…" Morgan placed a soft kiss to Jamie's temple and stroked a hand along Jamie's back. "Just relax, boy. No one else exists right now except us."

One word sat on the tip of Jamie's tongue, but he fought it. This man made him want things, feel things, he'd never thought he ever would. He rested his head on Morgan's lightly-haired chest and traced patterns on the man's skin with his fingertips. The silence between them stretched on, not uncomfortable but definitely thick with things Jamie wasn't sure how to even say.

"Move in with me."

Jamie stilled his hand. He didn't look up, but he felt Morgan's gaze on him nonetheless. "Why?"

"Because I want you here," Morgan said. "I'm that selfish."

Jamie chuckled. It wasn't a lie, but it didn't feel bad either.

"And you're safe here," Morgan continued. "I'd rather you be here than any of us worry about my best friend having to arrest me for beating the shit out of your father and brother."

"You have a point," Jamie said. He finally looked up, and, sure enough, Morgan was watching him. "I've never lived with anyone before except my family."

"There will be adjustments we'll both have to deal with," Morgan said. "It's just the way things go."

"Have you ever lived with anyone?"

"I have. I've been in a few long-term relationships. For various reasons, they never stuck. I think my past lovers, save for one, found me too controlling and intense."

Jamie snorted. "You are." He shifted upward enough for a kiss.

Morgan opened for him without hesitation. There was no fight for dominance or anything like it. Jamie felt himself slip away just a little bit more, and the notion wasn't quite as terrifying as it had been in Nashville. With Morgan, he felt safe and wanted.

"You, boy, are dangerous," Morgan murmured.

"How?"

Morgan pulled back enough for their gazes to meet once more. He stroked a fingertip along Jamie's jaw. "You make me want more than I think you realize."

Jamie swallowed. He hadn't a name to put to it in Nashville. He'd only known he would never find someone like Morgan ever again. He hadn't been able to get the man out of his head.

Laughter from the kitchen broke the spell before Jamie could get too lost in his thoughts.

Morgan smiled and kissed him. "Come on, boy. Let's get dressed and go see our houseguests."

Chapter Ten

Morgan settled on the couch, and Austin sat in the recliner. Chatter drifted in from the kitchen where Jamie and Jared cleaned up. Morgan hadn't argued when they both had insisted, and it gave him time to chat with Austin.

"The only one at the house was Aida," Austin said. "She'd come home, found a few broken items, other things scattered. Hell, she was on the phone with the station when I pulled up. She doesn't know where Daryl is."

Morgan sighed and let his head fall back. "What about Harlan?"

"He wasn't there, but I can't imagine he's going to be happy about it," Austin said. "And I don't mean the fight."

"Bastard probably knows where Daryl is. How is Aida handling this?"

"She's upset, and rightfully so."

"Do we have any idea where Daryl might be?" Morgan asked.

Jamie and Jared joined them a moment later. Jamie curled up on the couch against Morgan, while Jared sat at the other end, closer to the recliner. Morgan didn't miss the shy smile Jared gave Austin, or the almost-possessive look in Austin's blue eyes.

"My brother could be at Sam's," Jamie said.

"Sam?" Austin asked, turning his attention to Jamie. "Who is that?"

65

"Daryl's best friend. He lives down the road from us, well, from my folks' place. He's just as bad as Daryl, though not physical about it."

Austin nodded. "Definitely a possibility. Do you know the address?"

"No, but I can point out the house," Jamie said.

Morgan wanted nothing more than to object -- vehemently -- to the idea of Jamie going anywhere near that area now, but he bit his tongue. They didn't have a lot of choices. "I close the clinic at five. Austin, can you meet us there around then?"

"Sure. I'll follow you out there, but then you just keep going when I stop." Austin shook his head. "This isn't going to be pleasant by any stretch of the imagination. I can't see Harlan taking it without a fight."

"Feel free shoot them," Jamie muttered.

Morgan held him a bit tighter. "We will get through this, boy," he said, kissing Jamie's head where it tucked under his chin. When he glanced up, he noticed Jared watching them with nothing short of longing. Morgan caught Austin watching Jared and bit back a chuckle. It was only a matter of time. "How about we settle in for a movie before bed?"

Jamie nodded. "I'm game."

"Me, too," Jared said. He smiled at Austin, and Morgan swore his friend melted into the recliner. "Are you going to watch it with us, Officer Russell?"

"Of course," Austin said. "And, please, call me Austin."

Jared bit his lower lip, and his sweet, youthful face pinked. Morgan watched Austin shift a little in his chair. Yep, the man was thoroughly, utterly caught. Hook, line, and sinker.

"So, movies," Morgan said in an attempt to break the thick tension before his best friend pounced on Jared right there in the living room. "Ideas?"

"Something funny," Austin said. "I think we could all use a bit of humor."

Jamie snorted but didn't move from his position. "Police Academy."

Jared squeaked and half-kicked Jamie's foot. "Shh."

Morgan chuckled and grabbed the remote. "Something tells me there's a story here."

Jared groaned and got up. "Popcorn. You have popcorn?"

"I do indeed, top left cabinet beside the fridge," Morgan said. He nudged Jamie as soon as Jared headed for the kitchen. "Spill it, boy."

Jamie snickered and sat up a little. "Jared has a uniform fetish," he whispered, though he directed the comment at Austin. "Specifically, cops."

Austin grinned. "I see…"

Morgan just shook his head. "Go help him in the kitchen."

Jamie twisted around for a kiss. "Yes, Daddy."

His eyes widened, and his breath stopped for the briefest moment. He stared at Morgan.

Morgan smiled and cupped the back of his boy's head, tugging Jamie close. "My perfect boy," he murmured before taking a kiss.

Jamie's soft moan settled somewhere deep inside Morgan, and the feeling remained when Jamie got up to help Jared in the kitchen.

"You, my friend, are absolutely smitten."

It took considerable effort for Morgan to drag his attention from the kitchen to Austin, but he managed it. "I am." Morgan raked a hand through his hair. "He has no idea how much. Hell, Austin, I don't think I could ever put it into words."

"You love him."

It wasn't a question. Morgan nodded anyway.

"From the moment I saw him in Nashville, I knew I was well and truly hooked."

Austin smiled. "I don't think I've seen you like this in a long time. It's a good look. He's sweet, maybe a bit feisty, but not like folks seem to think."

"He's perfect," Morgan said. "For me, anyway."

* * *

"Asshole."

Jamie grinned and took out two bowls for the popcorn. "What?"

Jared glared at him. "Did you really have to suggest a cop movie?"

Shrugging, Jamie set the bowls on the counter beside the microwave. "Dude, Austin likes you. You like him. What's stopping you from going for it?"

"Nerves," Jared said, glancing at the doorway leading into the living room. "He's… intimidating. Sexy as hell, but a little scary, too."

"He won't hurt you," Jamie pointed out. The microwave dinged, and Jamie poured the first bag of popcorn into a bowl. Then he put the second bag in and started it.

"It's not that." Jared chewed on his lower lip. "I think he may be like Morgan," he whispered.

"You mean a Daddy Dom?"

Jared nodded.

Jamie turned his friend to face him fully. "In that respect, I totally get it. Morgan is… well, intense doesn't begin to cover it. But he also is very caring, loving."

Jared smiled slowly. "You're in love with him, aren't you?"

Was he? Jamie had never been in love, but this didn't feel like the crushes he'd had in the past. It felt far stronger. "I think so," he admitted. "Honestly, I don't know. I've never been in love, so I don't know if that's what this is. Besides, who's to say he feels the same?"

One of Jared's eyebrows rose. "That man looks at you like…" He shook his head. "Like you're his *everything*, like he's a starving man and you're the banquet spread out for him alone."

"But… isn't it too soon?" Jamie asked. "I mean, we haven't known one another even two weeks yet."

Jared crossed his arms. "My folks met and married three weeks later. They've been together for over thirty years. Love at first sight *is* a thing, you know."

The microwave dinged, and Jamie emptied the bag into the second bowl. "I know. I just don't want to fuck this up."

"Trust me, you won't. Now, what does Morgan drink?"

"He drank water during dinner, so I guess that," Jamie said. "What about Austin?"

"Pepsi." Jared grabbed three cans of Pepsi out of the fridge. Then he filled a glass with cold water from the pitcher. He cradled the cans in one arm and held the glass with the other before following Jamie back into the living room.

Jamie put the bowls on the coffee table, and Jared set down their drinks.

Morgan waited until Jamie settled against him again before starting the movie. Instead of sitting on the end of the couch, though, Jared sat on the floor at the end of the table, closest to the recliner. Jamie smiled as Austin stroked Jared's hair in thanks for the Pepsi.

Morgan fed Jamie popcorn throughout the movie, and, occasionally, Jamie caught Austin doing the same to Jared. Jamie smiled and snuggled closer to Morgan. He didn't want the night to end.

Chapter Eleven

"Thank you for this."

"Hey, no need to thank me. I've known Harlan all my life. I don't trust him as far as I can throw him. Now let's get your things out. Morgan's probably pacing his office right now."

Jamie stared out the windshield of Austin's patrol car and nodded. Of course, Daryl's car wasn't in the driveway or yard, but Dad's was. Sighing, Jamie got out, as did Austin. Before they even reached the front door of the trailer, it opened.

"Boy, I oughta --"

"Now, Harlan, I'm only gonna say this once," Austin interrupted, hand raised. "Jamie is here to gather his belongings, and that's it."

"That boy's a fucking menace!"

Jamie's gut twisted into knots. He really didn't want to go in there, but at least he wasn't alone. "Just please let me get my stuff."

His father scowled but stepped aside for them to enter the trailer. Jamie gave him a wide berth and headed for the tiny bedroom. He didn't have much, really, so it didn't take long to put it all into a big plastic bin and a couple of garbage bags. Mama stood in her bedroom doorway, her expression pained. Jamie spotted traces of tears, but there was nothing he could do. Dad and Daryl weren't nasty or even remotely mean to her, though Jamie had the feeling his dad cheated regularly. Not even Jamie's sisters came under fire. No, Jamie was the only one who'd managed to get caught in the homophobes' radars.

Mama grabbed one bag, and Austin took the bin. Jamie carried the other bag, and the three of them stepped out of the trailer. Just before they reached the patrol car, Daryl pulled into the driveway, effectively blocking Austin's car.

"The fuck?" Daryl growled. He stumbled out of his car, clearly drunk.

Austin put the bin in the trunk of his car and motioned for Mama and Jamie to put the bags in as well. "Call Morgan," Austin whispered to Jamie. "He needs to come get you."

Jamie moved out of the way and pressed number three on his favorites list.

"Jamie?"

"Hey, um, Daryl just pulled up," Jamie said. "Austin told me to call you to come get me. Daryl is drunk, so I think Austin is going to take him for driving."

"Got it," Morgan said. "I'm on my way."

Jamie hung up and watched as Austin approached Daryl.

"Good evening, Daryl," Austin said with a nod. "You have anything to drink tonight?"

Daryl spat on the ground to the side and sneered. "Ain't drivin' now."

"Doesn't matter," Austin said. He grabbed something out of the car, and Jamie realized it was a breathalyzer. "Gonna have you blow into this right quick."

Daryl scowled, gaze shifting to Jamie. "Why don't you have the faggot blow?"

"Now, Daryl," Austin said, an unnerving hint of steel in his voice. "We can do this easy or not."

Daryl actually blew into the device. Jamie figured it was merely protocol since even an idiot could've seen Daryl was ten sheets to the wind. Then the asshole lunged for Austin. Before Jamie realized what was happening, his brother was on the ground, face down, shouting and fighting as Austin cuffed him.

"So, in addition to the drinking and driving, we're gonna add assault on a law enforcement officer, got it." Austin got up and pulled Daryl to his feet as well. "You're making this easy, you know." He put Daryl into the backseat of his patrol car and dusted off his uniform. "Morgan on the way?"

Jamie nodded. Beside him, Mama stood, mouth agape. Dad still waited in the doorway of the trailer, his expression unreadable.

"Good." Austin turned his attention to Mama. "Mrs. Frost, do you feel safe enough here?"

"Yes," Mama said, her voice shaky. "Jamie's the only…"

Jamie hugged her while she cried, and he glared at his father. Harlan just stepped inside and shut the front door. "Mama, I'm okay."

She looked up at him, eyes full of fresh tears. "Where will you go?"

"I'm moving in with Morgan Sears."

"Dr. Sears? But why…" Her eyes widened in realization. "Oh."

"It started when Jared and I went to Nashville. He's good to me, Mama. And… I love him."

Mama took a shaky breath and nodded. "I know he is. Be careful, baby."

"I will," Jamie said. A car pulled up and parked along the side of the road. "That's Morgan." Jamie kissed Mama's cheek. "I love you."

She sniffled but smiled. "I love you, too. Please keep in touch."

"We live in the same town, not a problem." Jamie walked her to the trailer's front door. "If you feel like you have to leave, please call me."

"I will." She patted his cheek and went inside.

Jamie returned to the patrol car, dutifully ignoring the death glares he got from his asshole brother. He shook Austin's hand.

"Thank you for driving me out here."

Austin gestured toward the car. "No need to thank me, especially now that your idiot brother pretty much sealed his fate for the foreseeable future. Go on, Morgan's waiting and no doubt ready to murder the men in your family. I'll bring your stuff over after I get this moron booked."

Jamie shot his brother one last glare before heading to Morgan's car. As soon as he got in and buckled, he let his head fall back against the seat.

"Please take me home," he muttered.

"Gladly."

He stared out the window the entire ride to Morgan's place. Well, his place, too, now. Neither of them said a word until Morgan parked and the garage door shut behind them.

"Come on, boy," Morgan said, patting Jamie's thigh. "Let's eat dinner and settle in for the night."

Jamie nodded and got out. He followed Morgan inside and closed the door. When he turned, he found himself crowded between the door and Morgan, the man's hard kiss chasing away everything else. Jamie wanted nothing more than to lose himself in this man all over again. He slipped a hand between them and stroked the hardening ridge of Morgan's cock. In answer, Morgan pressed into his hand with a groan.

"Can I suck you?" Jamie asked in between breathless kisses.

"You never need to ask." Morgan stepped back, but instead of going to the bedroom, he simply opened his slacks right there in the mudroom. "On your knees, boy."

Jamie sank down and breathed in Morgan's scent. It sent his mind reeling, the smell of soap, cologne, and man all going right to his balls. Morgan lowered his boxers enough to free his cock. Jamie licked the head and drew it into his mouth. He'd seen it done so many times in porn, had chicks do it to him a few times in the past, but he'd never tasted another man until now.

"That's it, boy," Morgan said, one hand resting on the back of Jamie's head. "We'll work you up to taking it all, but, for now, just take what you can. Suck on the head."

Jamie did, and he felt the full-body shiver that ran through Morgan. Knowing he could draw out such a reaction from this man emboldened him. He lifted his gaze to meet Morgan's as he began sucking and bobbing his head. Morgan's stare felt like a fucking brand, and the man's hips quickened as he thrust in and out of Jamie's mouth.

"Fuck," Morgan muttered. His grip tightened on Jamie's hair. "Love an obedient boy."

Something between pride and adoration flushed through Jamie, making him even more eager to do his best.

"Hands behind your back," Morgan ordered him. Jamie did so, clasping his fingers. Morgan groaned, and the thrusts sped up. "Fuck… that's it… swallow Daddy's come, boy."

It was all the warning Jamie had before thick, warm semen shot down his throat. He whimpered and swallowed every drop. Morgan pulled out slowly and helped him to stand, surprising him with a deep, soul-consuming kiss.

"God, I love you," Morgan whispered on Jamie's lips.

Jamie nodded and draped his arms around Morgan's neck. "Love you, too, Daddy."

Jared Haley has been lusting after Officer Austin Russell since meeting the man in the woods one day. Virgin or no, Jared has done more than enough research to know exactly what he wants: a Dom.

Austin Russell knows it's only a matter of time before he gets his hands on Jared Haley. When he finally does, he knows he's found the sub meant for him.

Life, though, decides to throw them both — and their friends — a curve ball or two. Now they just need to figure out how to navigate it all.

Chapter One

Jared Haley dropped into one of the tiny, two-person booths and sighed. Head back, eyes closed, he took the chance to breathe. Mornings were always hell. Apparently, people in Sawyer didn't believe in cooking their breakfasts, so they descended en masse onto the town's only decent restaurant: Carl's Diner. The tips were good, but, damn, his feet hurt like hell, and he still had another two hours to go.

"You look like hell."

Jared opened his eyes as his best friend, Jamie Frost, sat across from him. "I've been here since five."

Jamie grimaced and slid a glass of Pepsi over. He sipped on another. "Why do you stay here? The money can't be that good."

"It's not that bad, either," Jared argued. He took a drink and studied the diners filling the restaurant. He hadn't been able to take a break to eat, and he doubted he would. His stomach grumbled in protest, but he chose to ignore it.

"You need to eat," Jamie said.

"I don't have time. Besides, you know Carl. 'If you're idle, there's work to be done.' Or whatever." Jared shrugged. "Either way, I have to get back on the floor. We had another call-out, so it's just me and… whatever the new chick's name is. I forgot."

"You realize he's supposed to give you an uninterrupted, thirty-minute break since you're working over six hours, right? And you've been here…" Jamie looked at his phone. "Seven hours now."

"I really don't want to rock the boat," Jared said. "We need the money."

Jamie sighed and sat back in his seat. "What happened?"

Jared swallowed and stared out the window beside the booth. "Mom left."

A fingertip touched the top of his hand, and he looked back at Jamie.

"I'm sorry. When?"

"About three this morning, before I got up. She left a note saying she was done and not coming back."

"How's your dad?"

"When I left for work at four, he was well into his bottle. He worked so hard to get sober over this past year. I don't really blame Mom for leaving, but it still fucking hurts."

"Jared!"

Jared sighed and pushed his almost-full glass to Jamie. "I have to get back to it."

"If you need me, I'll be here. Morgan's meeting me for lunch."

Nodding, Jared headed to the kitchen. Carl, the owner, waved him toward the pick-up window. Jared grabbed the tray and carried it back out to the dining room. He hadn't taken the order, but that didn't mean he couldn't get it to the table. He started for the diners and groaned.

Harlan Frost and his brother Mitchell sat with a couple of other men, all of whom sneered when Jared neared them. Jared set out their plates.

"Can I get you gentlemen anything else?" Jared asked in his best, feigned customer service voice.

One of the men looked him up and down, and Jared suppressed a shudder. "I thought waitresses wore skirts."

Jared bit his tongue. He needed this damned job. "I'll leave you to it."

He walked back toward the kitchen, not missing the cackles coming from Harlan's table. He spotted Jamie scowling at them and prayed his friend wouldn't let his temper get away with him. Harlan and Mitchell might've been Jamie's dad and uncle, but there was absolutely no love between them.

Jared took a second to gather some semblance of calm before he turned to go back out when he heard the bells over the diner door jingle. He pushed open the kitchen door to seat the newcomers.

Part of him wanted to smile. Another part of him wanted to hide in the kitchen.

Morgan Sears, the town's new doctor and Jamie's lover, stood at the door, but he wasn't alone. Sawyer's new police chief, Austin Miller, was with him. In full uniform.

Jared alternated between chills and full-blown inferno.

Gathing his wits, he went out to greet them. Jamie joined Morgan and Austin.

"Good afternoon, gentlemen," Jared said. He had to force himself to meet Austin's gaze. "If you'll follow me."

Thankfully, Harlan and his friends didn't make a sound when Jared walked by them. Jared dreaded what they were whispering amongst themselves, though. Most of it was probably directed at Jamie, to be honest. After Austin had arrested Jamie's brother, Daryl, tensions within the Frost family had skyrocketed.

Jamie slid into the booth, and Morgan sat beside him. Austin took the other side.

"How has the morning gone?" Austin asked, discreetly tipping his head back toward Harlan's booth.

"It's been… hell, to be honest."

"They giving you shit?" Austin asked.

"When are they not?" Jared shook his head. "I'm used to it. They're frequent customers, and Carl doesn't give a shit so long as they pay."

"When are you off?" Morgan asked him.

"Two. We had a call-out, and the new server is worse than Jamie ever was," Jared said with a wink at his best friend.

Jamie flipped him off. "Asshole."

"Boy," Morgan rumbled.

Jamie slumped a little, looking like a scolded child. "Sorry, Sir," he whispered.

The whole exchange made Jared chuckle. It was a bit of brightness in his otherwise hellish day.

"You guys want your usuals?"

"Sure thing," Austin said. "When do you go on break?"

Jared met Jamie's gaze, praying his friend kept his mouth shut. "Uh, I…"

Before he could finish, Carl shouted for him from the kitchen. Thankful for the interruption for once, Jared gave them an apologetic smile.

"I'll be right back with your drinks."

Chapter Two

The second Jared disappeared into the kitchen, Austin turned his attention to Jamie. "What the hell was that about?"

Jamie didn't seem like he wanted to say anything, but a glare from Morgan had him spilling it all. "Jared doesn't usually get breaks. Carl generally doesn't allow them."

Morgan's eyebrows nearly hit his hairline. "Excuse me?"

Austin had to reign in the urge to go back there and beat the shit out of the diner's slave-driving owner. "How long has Jared been working today?"

Jamie bit his lower lip. "Since five this morning."

"And he's not off until two?" Austin asked. Jamie nodded, and Austin started to get up. Jamie's hand caught him. "It's *illegal*, Jamie."

"Jared needs the job. His mom left the family this morning," Jamie said. "She got tired of his dad not holding a job, so she walked out. With his sister Renee gone, too, it's just Jared and his dad. They need the money."

Austin closed his eyes and counted to ten in his head. He only opened them when he sensed someone beside the table. He met Jared's shy gaze. "You have any office or computer experience?"

* * *

Jared blinked as he set their drinks down. "What?"

"I need help in the office," Morgan said. "Basic data entry and filing. I can guarantee you much better pay and safer working conditions."

"Um…" Jared wasn't sure what to say, honestly. He looked around the diner where he'd been working since high school. He turned back to Morgan. "Computer, yes, but I've never worked in an office."

"Easy enough to teach," Morgan said. "My receptionist will also make a good mentor."

Chewing on the corner of his bottom lip, Jared thought about the offer. "When could I start?"

Morgan and Austin both placed enough money to cover the drinks on the table. Then Austin put a twenty-dollar bill in Jared's hand, curling Jared's fingers over it.

"Now." Morgan stood, Jamie sliding out behind him.

Austin got up as well. "I'll walk him down to the clinic."

Jared watched Morgan and Jamie leave the diner, not missing the way Jamie's father scowled after them. Jared looked up at Austin. "What… just happened?"

Austin grinned and put an arm around Jared's shoulders. "You got a new job. Anything you need from the back?"

"Yeah, my jacket."

"Come on then. I need to have a word with Carl."

Oh, God.

As Jared led Austin into the kitchen, it felt like every single eye was on them. He shoved back the urge to hide and bypassed the main grill area to get his jacket.

"Boy!" Carl shouted. "What the hell are you —"

Austin rounded the corner, and Carl stopped short of grabbing Jared's arm. "If you so much as *touch* him, I'll make damn sure the Department of Labor knows how you stiff your employees of their legally-protected breaks."

Carl went absolutely white as a sheet.

"Now, I'm going to say this one time, and one time only." Austin stepped closer, and Carl backed up toward the grill where the cooks watched with wide eyes. "If an employee works over six hours, by law, they are allowed one thirty-minute break. The only exception is when there are ample opportunities during downtimes in between rushes. Do I make myself crystal clear?"

Carl nodded.

"Furthermore, you are responsible for protecting your employees from harassment at the hands of guests and other employees. So unless you want to lawyer up and face Jared Haley in court for failure to act when he's being mercilessly harassed while he works, then I highly suggest you reassess your priorities as a business owner and employer. Understood?"

When Carl tried to look at Jared, Austin snapped his fingers in front of the man's face, making Carl jump.

"*I* am speaking here," Austin said with steel in his voice. "You will not say another word to him." He leaned close, voice lowering. "*Ever.*"

Mouth open, Jared stood and watched Carl cower. Then Austin took Jared's hand in a gentle but sure grip.

"Come on. You're done here, boy."

Jared let Austin lead him through the dining room and out the front door. When he glanced back, Jared couldn't help but chuckle at the sight of Carl scrambling to attend to the diners.

"I wouldn't worry about them," Austin said as he put his hat back on. "He makes enough to get his head out of his ass and hire another server or two."

Jared shrugged. "I'm not really worried, to be honest. Carl is an asshole." He glanced over at Austin. Between the way Austin put Carl in his place and all those muscles wrapped up in a police uniform, Jared knew he'd be jerking off all night long.

Austin flashed him a cryptic smile and opened the clinic door when they reached it. Instead of leaving, though, he walked inside, too. He slipped off the hat and nodded to the receptionist.

"Good afternoon, Teresa. How are you today?"

"Hi, Officer Russell. I'm doing really well." She turned her bright smile to Jared. "Jared, right? Dr. Sears said you'd be by soon. I moved the spare laptop into the lab area. If you want to have a seat, I'll show you around and how to navigate the electronic records system when I'm done with reminder calls."

"Thanks," Jared said.

Austin crooked a finger, beckoning Jared down the hall. Teresa was already on the phone, so Jared followed his walking wet dream. Austin flicked on the light to what Jared realized was the lab room. Then Austin sat on a stool.

"We've been flirting since the day I met you in the woods."

Jared looked down the hall, then back to Austin. He nodded.

"Come here, boy."

The moment Jared was within reach, Austin gripped his hand and tugged him close. Jared's heart pounded, and, God, his cock practically begged for anything Austin would give him.

"Tell me now: yes or no?"

"Yes," Jared whispered, utterly breathless and lost in the man's blue eyes. "God, yes."

One kiss.

One kiss was all it took to set a fire in Jared's blood. He moaned softly into Austin's mouth as the cop's tongue stroked his own. Hands speared through Jared's hair and tilted his head, allowing Austin to practically devour him. Only the need for air ended the kiss. Jared stared into those eyes, breathless and hard as steel. God, he was screwed.

"Morgan closes the office at five." Austin took out his keys and removed one of them. He placed it in Jared's hand. "I won't be home until about six. I live right next door to him. Make yourself at home. The security code is 72778."

Jared studied the key and then looked back up at Austin. "Can I ask you something?"

"Of course."

Taking a deep breath, Jared figured he'd just get it out there in the open. "Are you like Morgan, a DaddyDom?"

Austin smiled. "In a sense, yes. I'm not a Daddy… but I am a Dom."

Jared swallowed. Yep. He was so utterly, wonderfully screwed.

"How does that make you feel?"

He took Austin's hand and pressed it against his hard cock. Austin chuckled, and Jared's knees nearly gave way when the man squeezed him through his pants. Jared gasped and held onto Austin's broad shoulders, going up on his tiptoes.

"Then we have some things to discuss tonight, boy. For now…" Austin squeezed just a bit harder, making Jared's heart skip a beat. "No touching this and no coming."

"Y-yes, Sir," Jared murmured.

"Good boy. I'll see you tonight."

Chapter Three

"Oh, my God. I would've killed to see that!"

Jared chuckled and unlocked the front door of Austin's house. "It was… fucking amazing, dude. The look on Carl's face was absolutely perfect."

Jamie laughed, and Jared thought he heard a door shut in the background. "Fucker deserved it, too."

"Agreed."

Jared stepped inside, then shut and locked the door behind him. He found the security system keypad and entered the number Austin had given him. There was a beep, and then the display flashed.

"Wow…"

"What?" Jamie asked. There were more noises in the background, pots and pans from the sound of it.

"Have you seen Austin's house yet? It's gorgeous." Jared set his keys on the small table in the foyer and wandered into the living room. Spacious, open, with a recliner and a massive plush sectional sofa dominating the room. A big-screen TV hung on one wall, and a brick fireplace was on the outermost wall.

"I haven't," Jamie said, making more noise, "but Morgan has."

"What the hell are you doing over there?"

"Cooking!"

"Gimme a sec. I need to cue up 911."

"Oh, fuck you," Jamie said with a laugh. "Morgan's been teaching me. Tonight's just a soup and sandwich night, so there's not a lot to do."

"You're making an insane amount of racket for 'soup and sandwiches,' you know."

"Oh! Daddy's home! Later, dude!"

Rolling his eyes, Jared stared at his phone for a moment when Jamie hung up. He always thought he'd be the one to wind up in a Daddy/boy situation, but Jamie needed it desperately. Morgan kept him grounded and out of trouble, and Jamie's temper had begun to improve.

Jared walked through the living room into a dining room. It wasn't a large area, and a bar separated it from the kitchen. He explored the kitchen itself, running a hand over the smooth top of the range. He could totally picture making meals in here. He wondered if maybe Austin would let him.

Beyond the kitchen, he went out into the hallway that extended from the foyer toward the rest of the house. Across from the living room was what seemed to be an office, judging by the enormous wooden desk, tall-backed chair, desktop PC, and various bookshelves. He couldn't help but browse the titles. Most of them were, unsurprisingly, crime thrillers, but there were also quite a few science fiction titles.

He left the office and found the laundry room across from the kitchen. Down the hall, he discovered a half bathroom with just a toilet and a sink. There was another room with a bed, but it didn't strike him as Austin's. That left one other door, which was closed. He thought about opening it, but then he stopped. Although it was a given what they would eventually do, he felt weird peering into Austin's room. He walked back down the hall instead and returned to the kitchen.

A pot rack hung over a center island, and every large appliance was made of dark steel. Despite feeling a little creepy opening cabinets, he did so anyway. The pantry was a massive closet beside the side-by-side fridge. He shut the door and returned to the living room.

Austin had told him to make himself at home, and the cushions on the couch looked incredibly inviting. Just a quick nap since Austin would be home in an hour.

* * *

Something soft on his lips woke Jared. He blinked up at a hunk in a cop's uniform.

"Hey."

"Hi, yourself," Austin said. He sat down on the edge of the wide cushion beside Jared. "How are you feeling?"

Jared yawned and stretched. "A bit more rested than I was, to be honest. What time is it?"

"About fifteen after six." Austin ran his fingers through Jared's hair, and Jared closed his eyes. "Are you hungry?"

Jared nodded. "Actually, I wanted to ask if I could fix dinner." He opened his eyes to find Austin watching him curiously. "What?"

"You worked your ass off, and yet you still want to cook?"

"I love cooking," Jared said with a shrug. "When I applied to Carl's in eleventh grade, it was for a cook position. I got stuck with being a waiter."

"Tell you what," Austin said as he got up. He held out a hand to Jared and helped him up as well. "If you want to cook, I won't stop you. I do, however, want to talk. Think you can focus on both?"

"Of course."

Austin smiled and pulled him closer for a soft kiss that made Jared's heart skip a beat. "Good. Come on."

Jared didn't want it to end, but his stomach grumbled, reminding him he hadn't eaten in hours. Austin held onto his hand and led the way into the kitchen. Then he pulled a stool out from under the bar and gestured toward the pantry and fridge.

"Anything in particular?" Jared asked. "First thing to consider is protein. Then I can build the rest of the meal around it."

"Surprise me," Austin said. "I'm all yours."

Jared shot him a grin. "You know, that can be taken in so many ways."

The expression on Austin's gorgeous face changed to something much more lewd, and he stood. Before Jared could blink, the man had him pinned against the fridge door, that muscular body so much stronger, taller, broader than his own. Jared's heart pounded, and he stared up into blue eyes that made him weak in the knees.

"Feed me, boy," Austin said, his voice low, husky, and threaded with all sorts of promises. "Then I will show you just how I plan on *taking* you."

Jared wanted, more than anything, to sink to his knees and find out if giving a blowjob was as good as it looked in porn. "Sir…"

Austin bent and kissed him, tongue thrusting into Jared's mouth and thoroughly scrambling every single thought in Jared's brain. Then he ended it slowly and stepped back with a wink. Jared had to lean against the fridge to remain upright.

"Food first, boy. Then play."

Nodding, Jared watched him go sit back down. Food. Right. He could do this.

Chapter Four

Austin found he enjoyed watching Jared cook. The young man moved around the kitchen as if he'd been born to do it. They'd decided on tilapia since it was quick to thaw out, so that's what Jared was cooking. According to him, rice pilaf and greens made great sides to go with it. Austin was happy to let him go for it.

"Will talking distract you?"

Jared smiled over at Austin as he thawed the filets under running water. "Nope."

Austin nodded. "All right. First off, and I don't ask this to embarrass you, but are you a virgin?"

"Yes, I am," Jared said. He didn't seem the least bit self-conscious about it, thankfully. "In all honesty, I've only kissed one person: Jamie. We figured out fast that we weren't going to work like that. In terms of sex, I've jerked off, obviously, and I've only used my fingers."

Austin resisted the urge to adjust himself in his pants. Just the notion of watching Jared finger himself while begging for a cock made Austin want to drag the young man to bed now. "Good to know."

Jared returned to the stove and readied the filets for the oven with seasonings and a brush of olive oil. Then he washed his hands and approached Austin. "I've watched a lot of porn, though." When Austin turned to the side, Jared stood between his legs, hands running up along Austin's thighs. "There are things I can't wait to do, Sir."

Austin groaned as those wandering hands neared his hard cock. "Boy…"

Jared leaned in for a soft kiss. Austin had absolutely zero chance of keeping it light and easy. He slipped off Jared's glasses, gripped Jared's head in both hands, and deepened the kiss, drowning in the moan Jared fed him. When he ended it, he stared into gorgeous, chocolate brown eyes.

"I want nothing more than to explore everything you learned in porn and teach you a whole lot more, but dinner and talking first. I know you've done research into the lifestyle. Do you know what a safeword is?"

Jared nodded. "I even picked one: skillet."

Austin smiled and stroked his fingers through Jared's hair. "Good boy. Let's get some food in us and chat."

Jared took another kiss and put his glasses back on. As he stepped back, he dragged his fingers along the hard ridge of Austin's cock. "Yes, Sir."

It took considerable effort to rein in the need to get his hands on Jared, but Austin somehow managed it. Jared returned to fixing their dinner, this time focusing on the rice pilaf. From scratch. Austin had no clue he had the *ingredients* to do that from scratch.

"I imagine you know that Morgan has very specific rules for Jamie."

"I do," Jared said as he started the rice. "Personally, I think Jamie needs them. Do you have rules?"

"I do, though they aren't all the same as Morgan's." Austin leaned on the bar, arms on top, and continued. "My biggest one involves orgasm control." He smiled when a tiny shiver slid through Jared's lean body. "How does that make you feel?"

Jared was silent for a moment before answering. "Honestly? Ungodly horny."

Austin chuckled. "Good. I don't write out my rules like Morgan either, but they are easy enough to remember. Number one, as stated, is orgasm control. You will come only when I allow it. If you come without permission, there *will* be a punishment. Number two is related to that: no touching yourself. Your cock and ass, indeed your whole body, are mine. You may ask for permission, but that doesn't mean you will get it. Any questions?"

"What about hygiene? Or is that a stupid question?" Jared asked him, glancing over.

"There are no stupid questions. Washing and using the restroom are given in terms of touching, but only as needed. When you wash, you wash and nothing more. Now, rule three may feel weird at the beginning, but you'll get used to it." At Jared's questioning expression, Austin grinned. "When you are in this house, you will be nude. The only time you are allowed clothing in here is when we have company and when you are cooking."

Jared blushed and bit his lower lip. "Yes, Sir. Should I undress when I'm done cooking?"

"Yes," Austin said. "Those are my primary rules. More may come up as we explore this, so keep that in mind. Do you have any questions for me so far?"

"Some of the things I saw and read online had subs kneeling, like at their Dom's feet when eating. Do you require that?"

"Not when we are eating," Austin said. "When we are watching television or simply relaxing, then yes."

Jared nodded and slid the sheet pan with the fish into the oven. He set the timer and checked on the rice without lifting the lid before turning to face Austin. "I don't have anymore questions… yet, Sir."

"Then it's time to discuss likes and dislikes," Austin said. "Hard limits are things you absolutely will not do. Soft limits are things you would like to try or enjoy. Favorites are just that: things you love."

"Hard limits… obviously nothing illegal, like animals, anyone under eighteen, dead things." He grimaced and shuddered. "Also no bodily wastes or blood. Beyond those, I don't know what I do or don't like yet."

Austin nodded. "That makes perfect sense. What about soft limits and faves?"

The blush crept into Jared's youthful face. "I love watching anything involving toys like dildos, vibrators, plugs. I always wanted to experiment, but I've never had the chance to." He turned when the timer went off and removed the fish from the oven. Then he moved the rice to the side and finished the pilaf.

"Have you ever given a blowjob?" Austin didn't miss the shiver and smiled. Jared shook his head without looking over as he plated their dinners. "Have you tasted yourself when you've jerked off?"

"Yes, Sir," Jared murmured as he turned around, plates in hand.

Austin pulled out a stool beside him and patted it. Jared set their plates down before retrieving silverware. "Grab two Pepsis."

Jared did and sat down beside Austin. "I hope you like it."

"I don't doubt it in the least." Austin took a bite of the fish. "Damn… why the hell are you not in school to be a chef?"

Jared shot him a shy smile before taking a bite as well. "Thank you, Sir. I'd love to be, but it's just not in the cards."

Austin made a mental note to look into it. "Back to our discussion… One of the first things a sub should know is how to give a proper blowjob. I won't make you deepthroat right away, but we *will* work up to it."

Jared's soft moan could've been due to the delicious food… or the knowledge of what Austin had in mind once they finished eating. Either way, it was sexy as sin.

"Yes, Sir."

Chapter Five

Jared put the dishes into the dishwasher, occasionally glancing toward the bar where Austin sat and checked emails. The conversation earlier lingered in Jared's mind, and his cock had yet to soften even the slightest bit. Just knowing what they'd be doing in a few minutes made him weak in the knees. When done, he went back to the bar.

Austin turned his phone to silent and set it on the bar. "Living room. We're going to have a bit of fun."

Not doubting that in the least, Jared followed him into the living room. Austin grabbed the remote and sat in the overstuffed armchair. Then he pointed to the floor between his legs.

"Strip and kneel, boy."

Jared wasn't generally self-conscious, but he couldn't tamp down the nervousness as he undressed. The last time he'd been nude in front of anyone, it had been a doctor years ago.

Austin's gaze slid up Jared's body from head to toe and back. With a nod from him, Jared knelt, putting him at eye-level with Austin's crotch. Smiling, Austin turned on the TV.

"Smart TVs are wonderful things. They can access all sorts of content online—including porn."

Jared bit his lower lip and glanced over one shoulder at the TV. Austin started up one that, judging by a few quick clips at the beginning, involved anal toy play. Naked, there was no way Jared could hide the raging hard-on now. Austin chuckled and set the remote down.

"Come here, boy." Austin beckoned Jared closer. He undid his pants, and a beautifully thick, hard cock pushed out into the cop's hand. Jared licked his lips. "Bring that pretty mouth here. Start with the head. Lick it, suck on it."

Jared set his glasses on the table by the chair, leaned in, and swiped his tongue over the head, catching a drop of precome. He'd tasted his own before, but it wasn't nearly as good as this. Austin groaned softly as Jared closed his lips around the crown and sucked. One hand held onto the base of Austin's cock, and the other gripped Jared's hair.

"That's it, boy," Austin muttered. "Breathe in through your nose when you slide down. Only go as far as you feel comfortable for now."

The porn sounds from the TV mixed with Austin's, filling the room with the most insanely erotic soundtrack on the planet. Jared put his hands on Austin's strong thighs and sucked the man's cock in as much as he could. He loved the way it flexed on his tongue and filled his mouth. Austin's hand in his hair tightened a little, and it made Jared's own cock ache for release.

"Fuck, you're good at that," Austin groaned. He pushed his hips upward while gently guiding Jared's head up and down. "Swallow on the downstroke." When Jared did, Austin grunted. "Yeah, like that. Fuck."

Jared's heart pounded, and he dug his fingers into Austin's thighs. He struggled to hold back the urge to come, but it lingered right there on the edge. Just when he thought he'd break the no-coming rule, Austin tugged his head up.

"I'll come in your mouth if you keep that up," Austin said, sounding just as close to the edge. "Get up here, boy."

As Jared stood, Austin opened up a drawer in the table. He grabbed a square package and a tube of lube. At Jared's chuckle, Austin winked up at him.

"I knew this would happen eventually. I was a Boy Scout—always prepared." Austin unrolled the rubber onto his cock and crooked a finger. "Straddle me. I want to get inside that sweet hole, boy."

Jared climbed up onto Austin's lap. Hands on Austin's shoulders, he shivered when Austin spread his asscheeks. Then a slick finger rubbed his hole, and he gasped.

"Shh… just my finger," Austin murmured.

It eased inside slowly, and Jared tried desperately not to fuck himself on it. God, it felt so fucking good. Austin worked it in and out, never looking away from Jared's eyes.

"More?"

Jared nodded. When a second finger pushed inside him, it sent a rush of heat through his entire body. Austin spread the two fingers apart and brushed something deep inside. Sparks of pure pleasure shot through Jared. "Sir," he gasped, eyes widening. "Oh, my God…"

Austin smirked and fucked him with both fingers. "Prostate. Feels good, doesn't it?" Jared moaned and nodded. "Need another? Or are you ready for my cock?"

"Cock," Jared moaned. If Austin's fingers felt this good, he couldn't wait to feel the man's dick.

Austin withdrew his fingers and gave himself a stroke to slick his cock. Then he lined up with Jared's hole. "Bear down as I slide in. Tell me if you need me to stop."

Whatever Jared wanted to say simply fled his brain as his ass stretched around the head of Austin's cock. Staring down into blue eyes, he began to shiver as the cop slowly filled him. By the time Austin's cock was fully inside, Jared's mind had shut off in favor of just *feeling*.

"Christ, you're so fucking tight," Austin groaned. His hands rested on Jared's hips. "Move when you're ready, boy. Just up and down."

His head swimming in the incredible sensations, Jared started gliding up and down, slow and easy. His eyes rolled with every stroke of Austin's cock in his ass. He'd never felt anything so utterly amazing in his life.

"That's it..." Austin whispered, though his voice sounded strained. "Fuck, I love being buried in your ass, boy."

In the background, the porn sounds continued, moans and grunts from the men on the TV only adding to the sounds Austin made. Jared's own pants and moans increased as he moved a bit faster. Austin's hands on his hips tightened.

"Hold it," Austin said. "Ride my cock like a good boy, but do not come."

Jared whimpered but nodded. "Y-yes, Sir. Oh, fuck…"

Austin chuckled and sped up his thrusts into Jared's ass. "Just like that. Yeah. You like my cock in your asshole?"

Jared gasped, unable to look away from the cop's blue gaze. "Sir!"

One hand left Jared's hip and grabbed the back of his head, jerking him down for a hard kiss. Austin growled into his mouth, and the cock buried in Jared's ass flexed and pulsed, filling the rubber with come.

"Now you may come."

Shouting, Jared ground onto Austin's lap, the cop's cock rubbing that spot inside him. Come spurted between them, splattering onto his bare torso and Austin's uniform shirt. Shaking, Jared collapsed onto him, head on Austin's broad shoulder.

Austin kissed his head and caressed his back. "Such a good boy," he murmured. "Let's get cleaned up and get in bed. Need to go home tonight?"

Jared drew in a shaky breath and shook his head. "Dad's probably passed out drunk. He won't notice if I'm not there."

Austin nodded and kissed the side of his head again. "Okay. Up, boy. Let me get you cleaned up. Then I want you in my bed and my arms."

Chapter Six

"Heard you quit your job."

"Good morning to you, too, Dad."

Jared put the mail on the tiny dining table and looked around the kitchen. He hadn't been home since yesterday morning, yet the sink alone looked like a bomb had gone off days ago. Sighing, he turned and headed into the living room, which was just as trashed. His father, Jack, watched him with bloodshot eyes as Jared began picking up trash.

Dad burped, and even from the other side of the room, Jared smelled whiskey. "Need money."

Rolling his eyes, Jared carried a handful of garbage to the trash can in the kitchen. Then he grabbed the can and dragged it to the living room. "Got a new job, better pay."

Dad grunted and tried to sit up. He only succeeded in spilling yet more trash onto the floor from the depths of his tattered recliner. "Where?"

"Dr. Sears' office," Jared said as he tossed garbage into the can. He picked up more empty beer cans than he recalled seeing on an entire aisle in the store. "How'd you hear about me quitting Carl's anyway?"

"Your uncle saw you walking down the road with a cop when you were supposed to be working."

Jared met his dad's gaze, and Dad's eyes narrowed.

"You in trouble with the law?"

"No. Nothing like that."

Dad let out a noise somewhere between a grunt and burp. "Why were you with a cop then?"

Standing straight and raking a hand through his hair, Jared contemplated lying. Being with Austin, though, made him happy, gave him hope for once. It also bolstered his courage. "We're dating."

Dad nearly fell out of his chair. "What?" he shouted.

Jared instinctively took a step back. Dad wasn't abusive, nor was he an angry drunk, but Jared had seen Jamie deal with enough shit that he had developed his own fight-or-flight response to raised voices.

Dad blinked and shook his head. "Sorry," he muttered. He waved toward the couch, and Jared sat down on the edge. Dad sighed and sank back into his chair again, raking a hand through his hair. "I'm not mad. I just worry, given what your friend has to deal with from his family. So… Officer Russell, huh?"

"Yeah," Jared said.

Dad nodded. "He good to you?"

"He is. He, uh, confronted Carl about my breaks issue. He also helped me get the job working for Dr. Sears."

"Good." Dad grimaced as he looked around the room, as if seeing it for the first time in several days. He sighed. "No wonder your mama left. I'm fucking hopeless."

"Dad…" Jared reached over and touched Dad's knee. "You're not hopeless. You just need help. You were sober for a year, and you can do it again."

Dad's head fell back against the chair, and he closed his eyes. "I know," he muttered. "I guess I need to start by getting a shower." He lifted one arm, sniffed, and nearly gagged. "Yeah. Shower."

With Jared's help, he got up and tottered a bit. Jared didn't let go of his arm until Dad nodded.

"Gimme a few, and I'll help you clean up in here." He glanced back at Jared before heading down the hall. "I'm sorry."

"No need to apologize, Dad. We'll get through it."

As Dad went to the bathroom, Jared pulled out his cell. He hit number one on speed dial.

"Hey," Jamie said. "Thought you were going home today."

"I am home. Dad was passed out in his recliner."

"Oh… everything okay?"

Jared sighed and scanned the disaster of their small house. "Yes… and no. He knows about Austin now, and he knows I don't work at Carl's anymore. He's actually okay with both."

"Really?" Jamie asked. "He's fine knowing you're gay?"

"Yeah. He even acknowledged he needs help getting sober again. Does Morgan have resources for alcoholics?"

"Probably," Jamie said. "I'll ask him. Wanna come over later?"

"If y'all don't mind," Jared replied. "Austin is working today."

"Tell ya what, just drop by when you can. Morgan doesn't open the office on weekends."

"Sounds good." Jared heard the bathroom door open. "Look, I need to get going. Will see you later."

"Okay."

Jared hung up and looked up to see his dad standing in the hallway. He seemed more refreshed now that he was showered and wearing clean clothes.

"Let's get this mess cleaned up," Dad said. "Then maybe have breakfast?"

Jared smiled and set his phone on the cluttered coffee table. "Works for me."

* * *

"So he's serious about getting back on the wagon?" Jamie asked.

Jared nodded and popped another fry in his mouth. "He is. He was doing so well until Mom left."

Jamie scowled and poked the ketchup on his plate with a French fry. "Bitch."

Smirking, Jared nodded. "No argument here. She was the one who didn't like you, ya know. Dad likes you, thinks you're a 'good kid,' his words."

Morgan chuckled and ruffled Jamie's hair as he walked by. "A very good boy."

Much to Jared's amusement, Jamie blushed.

"Thank you, Daddy."

Jared couldn't picture himself ever calling Austin that, but the dynamic perfectly suited Morgan and Jamie. Morgan sat down, and Jamie leaned over, head resting on Morgan's shoulder.

"You went home with Officer Russell last night," Jamie said with a grin.

"Yes, I did." Jared ate another fry and smiled.

"And…?"

"Boundaries, boy," Morgan said.

Jamie huffed. "But we're best friends."

"And Austin is *my* best friend," Morgan reminded him. "If they want to share details of their intimate moments, they will."

Jared winked at his friend. "It was fucking amazing."

Jamie grinned. "It really is, isn't it?"

Nodding, Jared took a bite of his burger. He swallowed, but before he could answer, a knock sounded on the front door. Morgan kissed Jamie's head and got up to answer it.

"Not a virgin anymore, huh?" Jamie whispered.

"Nope. God, Jamie… he's perfect."

A familiar voice came from the foyer, and then Morgan and Austin walked into the dining room. Morgan sat back down but nodded toward the kitchen.

"Your boy cooked dinner. There's an extra burger for you in the microwave."

Austin bent and kissed the top of Jared's head before getting his food. Then he sat down beside Jared. "So you've discovered how good he is."

"Indeed," Morgan said with a grin. He turned his attention to Jared. "Why aren't you in cooking school?"

"We couldn't afford it," Jared said with a shrug.

"Working on that."

Jared blinked over at Austin. "Wait. What?"

Austin winked at him. "Eat, boy. We'll talk about it later. Now, tell me how things went at home."

For the next twenty minutes, Jared told them about going home to find his dad passed out in the living room. Morgan nodded when Jared mentioned getting info to aid alcoholics. When Jared said his dad didn't care that he's gay, Austin put his arm around Jared's shoulders and squeezed.

"I'm glad," Austin said. "I have my hands full with the Frosts."

Jamie frowned. "I heard. Mama said Daryl and my dad have been grumbling about… something, but she doesn't know what."

"I know," Austin said with a sigh. "We've gotten a few tips from anonymous sources about them, so we're keeping watch. Don't worry."

Jared didn't like the sound of that, but he knew Austin could handle it.

Chapter Seven

Austin groaned and rubbed his temples. This whole mess just refused to die down. He looked up at Harlan Frost, who was currently ranting about how the town's doctor was taking advantage of Harlan's 'boy.' Tired and beyond ready to get the fuck out of here, Austin just held up his hand. Harlan, surprisingly enough, shut up.

"All right, first off, Jamie is a grown man." Austin scowled at Harlan when the man opened his mouth to respond. "I'm not done."

Harlan snapped his mouth shut.

"Second, the relationship between Jamie and Dr. Sears does not concern you. *At all.* Understood?"

"It's sick and unnatural."

Austin snorted. "You're entitled to your opinion, no matter how skewed it is, but no one is required to acknowledge it or agree with you."

Arms crossed, Harlan scowled. "You're just standing up for them because you're a f—"

"I highly suggest you rethink your words. *Fast,*" Austin said, gaze narrowed. "What people do in the privacy of their homes is no one's business. Do I make myself crystal clear? Furthermore, if you continue to harass Jamie or Jared, I will have you arrested. Understood? Now, if there's nothing else, I'm going to suggest you go home, focus on your family, and leave everyone else alone."

"He's my son!"

Austin stood slowly, hands flat on his desk. He was taller than Harlan by about half a foot. Idiot or not,

Harlan had the good sense to look cowed and shrank into his chair. "I'm going to say this one time: Jamie wants *nothing* to do with you. If you so much as step foot on Morgan Sears' property, you will be back here in cuffs. Now get out."

Harlan got up and stalked out of the station, muttering under his breath. Austin dropped back into his chair and grabbed his cell. He didn't even bother to say hi when someone picked up the other line.

"Remind me that I can't strangle someone."

Morgan chuckled. "Hello to you, too. Harlan, I assume."

"Who else?" Austin said with a sigh. "Have you talked to Jamie about a restraining order?"

"He agreed," Morgan said.

"Good. Get it done. I don't trust Harlan or Daryl as far as I can throw them."

"Noted. Jamie has been talking about finding work as well."

Austin looked around his office. There was very little staff for such a small station, but they could use someone to help with basic maintenance and cleaning. "Let me make a few calls. I might have an idea."

"I already know where this is going," Morgan said. "Personally, I love the idea. I keep an eye on yours, and you keep an eye on mine."

"Exactly. At any rate, I'm heading home. Jared still over there?"

"He is. Want me to send him to your place?"

"Yeah, but… would you two walk him over? I know it's next door, but Harlan's got my nerves all sorts of fucked."

"Absolutely. We'll get him home safe."

"Thanks. Talk to you later."

Twenty minutes later, Austin walked into the house and set his keys on the table near the door. He hung his hat up and went to the kitchen. He froze and licked his lips at the sight that greeted him.

Bent over, in jeans that should've been illegal, Jared was taking out a casserole dish from a lower cabinet. Austin wasted no time in sliding up behind him and pressing himself against that gorgeous ass. Jared gasped and straightened up.

"Now that was a sight any man would love to come home to," Austin whispered in Jared's ear.

Jared rubbed his butt against Austin and turned his head enough for a kiss. "I thought I'd get dinner started, Sir," he murmured on Austin's lips.

Austin reached out and removed the dish from Jared's hand. He set it on the counter and stepped back. With one hand on Jared's hip and the other on his upper back, Austin bent his lover forward until Jared was pressed into the countertop.

"I'm going to eat my dessert first."

Without giving Jared a chance to reply, Austin undid the young man's jeans and shoved them and Jared's underwear down. Then he crouched and kneaded Jared's asscheeks with both hands, exposing his boy's puckered hole.

The second his tongue touched that sweet, tight hole, Jared gasped. Austin licked and pushed inside, and Jared shivered. Austin reached around and gripped his boy's hardening cock, giving it a long, slow stroke.

"Oh, fuck," Jared moaned, hips beginning to rock between Austin's mouth and hand. "Sir…"

Austin pulled back long enough to say, "no coming, boy," before thrusting his tongue back inside.

Jared whimpered and moaned, whole body trembling as Austin feasted on his ass. Austin gave his lover's hole one more lick and stood. Jared's head landed on the counter, pillowed on his arms.

"Don't move," Austin said.

He patted Jared's ass and headed to the bedroom. He tugged his toy chest out of the closet and grinned as he opened it. He'd bought the small plug a week ago, knowing damn well he'd eventually get his hands on Jared. He grabbed it and the lube, then returned to the kitchen. Jared hadn't moved, but he watched Austin, eyes wide when he saw the plug.

"Oh, my God."

Austin smirked and set the toy on the counter beside Jared. Then he popped open the lube, slicked two fingers, and began easing them into Jared's ass. "If you come without permission, you won't be sitting comfortably for a few days." He angled his fingers and stroked them over Jared's gland.

"Sir!"

Austin chuckled and withdrew. Then he lubed the plug and positioned it at Jared's hole. "Bear down, boy. It's made for long-term wear."

The plug sank into Jared's ass, and he moaned. Austin made sure it was seated and tapped the base. Jared whimpered, hips moving again.

"Dinnertime," Austin said as he pulled Jared's pants and underwear back up. "Stay dressed until you're done cooking, then all clothes come off. We'll eat in the living room, but I'll feed you."

"Y-yes, Sir," Jared panted. "Oh, fuck. So full."

Austin helped him to stand up straight and turned him around for a kiss. "This is a small one, boy. I have much larger ones."

Jared blinked up at him, eyes wide. "Larger?"

Austin grinned, reached around, and patted Jared's ass over the plug. Jared yelped and pressed closer. "*Much* larger."

Chapter Eight

Jared knelt between Austin's legs and did his best to not squirm—too much. The plug wasn't too big, but considering he'd never worn one, it was difficult to ignore. Austin fed him bites of the chicken and rice casserole, all the while praising him on how good it tasted.

"Later, I'd like to talk about culinary school options."

"I wish I could do it, but we just don't have the money, Sir."

Austin smiled, fed Jared the last bite, and set the plate aside. "Like I said, we will discuss it later." He stood and helped Jared up as well. "Right now, I have other plans for you, boy. Bedroom."

Keeping hold of Jared's hand, Austin led the way down the hall to the bedroom. As soon as the door was shut, Austin steered him toward the bed.

"On the bed, on your back." Austin crawled onto the bed, spreading Jared's legs open as wide as possible. He caught Jared's hands and pressed them on the pillow above Jared's head. "Your hard-no list didn't include restraints."

"No, Sir," Jared murmured. His heart pounded at the thought of being unable to move while Austin did whatever he wished. His cock loved the idea even more. "Please?"

Austin grinned. "Don't move."

He got up and went to the closet. He rummaged in a chest, then returned with a set of leather wrist restraints. He took his place between

Jared's legs again and secured both of Jared's wrists in the restraints. Then he reached down between the headboard and the mattress for something. Jared heard metal on wood, and Austin hooked a chain to the short one connecting the cuffs.

"If you need out, use your safeword. Understood?" Austin asked.

Jared nodded. "Yes, Sir."

Austin leaned down to give him a kiss. Jared moaned into the man's mouth, whole body rocking when Austin pressed down onto him. Knowing Austin still wore his uniform only served to drive Jared's need higher. Austin chuckled and pulled back, blue eyes gazing into Jared's.

"Oh, believe me, boy," Austin said, his grin lascivious as hell. "I know all about your fetish."

Jared groaned and bit his lower lip. "Sir…"

Austin got up, slid his belt out of the loops, and dropped it to the floor. Then he unbuttoned his shirt but didn't remove it. He undid his pants and left them on. Then he got a couple of things from the chest near the closet. When he returned to the bed, Jared's eyes widened. Another set of restraints dangled from Austin's hand.

"Legs up close to your chest."

When Jared did, Austin secured the restraints around his thighs. Then he hooked them to a long bar that kept Jared's legs wide apart. Another two chains were attached to the wrist cuffs, keeping his legs up. Spread wide open and unable to move, Jared whimpered at the mere thought of what all Austin could do to him. His cock leaked precome onto his belly, and his plugged hole was on full display.

"Remember your safeword," Austin said.

"Y-yes, Sir," Jared muttered.

Smirking, Austin leaned over and picked up his belt from the floor. He wrapped it around his hand, leaving only a little bit of the leather end to hang free.

"Oh, God…"

"This is not a punishment," Austin said. "You've done nothing to warrant one. I won't make it too hard since it's your first time. I want to hear you, though. Every moan, every shout."

The first light snap made Jared's breath catch. It landed directly over his plugged hole, making him clinch. The second one hit his right asscheek, and he moaned softly. Then the left. He tried to arch up for more, but he couldn't move much. Austin snapped the belt end again, this one landing on the back of Jared's upper right thigh. Jared gasped, and his cock jerked.

"No coming, boy," Austin said. "Just a few more. Your ass looks so fucking hot with the marks."

Jared moaned when another strike managed to connect with the plug's base. "Sir…"

Another one hit the back of Jared's upper left thigh. Then the belt slapped across his ass again. He shouted and struggled not to come. His cock ached and leaked profusely.

"Sir! Close!"

Austin tossed the belt aside and removed the plug. Jared's eyes rolled when two slick fingers plunged into his hole. He moaned and desperately tried to angle his hips for more. Austin pushed in a third.

"Sir…" Jared panted as Austin worked him open. "Please!"

Chuckling, Austin got sheathed and thrust into him, going balls-deep in one stroke. Jared cried out and trembled. Austin held onto the backs of Jared's legs and took him hard and fast. Every thrust nailed that spot deep inside, and Jared jerked and tugged the restraints, so fucking close.

"Now, boy," Austin panted as he slammed into Jared over and over. "Come on my cock."

Jared cried out, entire body bowing as come spurted up onto his belly. Austin groaned and ground into him, and Jared felt the man's cock pulsing inside him.

Breathless, Jared could only shiver as Austin pulled out and released him from the restraints. Then Austin cleaned them both and collapsed onto the bed. He gathered Jared close and kissed his head while running one hand up and down Jared's back.

"That…" Jared struggled to catch his breath and gather his wits. "That was fucking amazing."

"Indeed, boy. Get some rest, and we can talk later. Do you need to go home tonight?"

Jared shook his head. "Dad knows where I am."

"He's okay with it?"

"He is." Jared kissed Austin's chest and draped his arm over the cop's torso. "I always had a feeling he knew I was gay and that he'd be okay with it. Mom, probably not so much."

"Do you want to talk about it?" Austin asked him.

"Not right now," Jared murmured. "Right now, I want to bask in the afterglow."

Austin chuckled. "Agreed."

Chapter Nine

"Hey, Jared," Teresa called from the lobby. "Someone's up here to see you."

Jared left his nook in the lab area and headed up front. He froze and stared at his mother. "Um… hi."

Margie Haley had always preferred to appear more affluent than she actually was, and now was no exception. One thing missing, however, was her wedding ring set. "I need to speak with you."

Jared told himself he wasn't going to make a scene, certainly not at work. He glanced at Teresa, who gave him with a sympathetic smile. "Will you let Dr. Sears know I'll be outside for a few minutes, please?"

"Of course. Take your time."

Nodding, Jared gestured for the front door. As soon as he and his mother were outside, he turned to her. "Why are you here?"

"I came back to retrieve some of my belongings from the house. I stopped at Carl's, but they said you quit." She shook her head. "Well, at least *you* got another job."

Jared crossed his arms and glared at her. "Go back to wherever you ran away to."

Her mouth popped open, and she stared at him. "Excuse me? I'm your mother, and that's no way to speak to me!"

It took more effort than he cared to admit, but Jared squared his shoulders. "You may have given birth to me, but that's it. When you walked out the door, you walked out of my life for good."

Margie gaped at him. "How dare you! You're just like your father, a worthless, pathetic fa—" She froze and stared at something over Jared's shoulder.

"Good afternoon, Mrs. Haley."

Jared resisted the urge to smile.

Austin, in full uniform, stepped up beside Jared and tipped his hat. "Is there a problem here?"

Margie snapped her mouth shut, but then she seemed to gather fresh fuel for her tirade. "Afternoon, Officer Russell. This is just a discussion between a mother and her son. Nothing more."

"Nothing, huh? I'm sure I heard you almost use a rather nasty slur." Austin put his arm around Jared's shoulders. "I don't think I need to explain why such a thing would be unwise."

Margie stood a bit straighter, and Jared almost laughed when she tilted her head just enough to make her look like the self-entitled snob she was. "Well. It seems you have made your… *bed*, Jared." Then she glared at them both. "Harlan was right about you two, and, no doubt, the *good* doctor and Jamie."

Jared narrowed his eyes at her. What the fuck did Harlan Frost have to do with this? He glanced up at Austin, but the cop just shook his head slightly.

"Unless you have something else to say to Jared, I'm going to assume you are done here," Austin said. "Now, I'm taking him to dinner, and then we are going home."

"His father would never—"

"Dad knows and is perfectly fine with it," Jared interrupted. "Furthermore, he has nothing to say to you."

"That house is—"

"All in his name," Jared said. "I've seen the papers. You have no claim to any of it. Get your shit and leave us alone."

Margie scowled and stalked away, back toward a suspiciously new car.

"Something's going on," Jared muttered as they watched her slide behind the wheel.

"Agreed. I think maybe Jamie, Aida, and your dad need to hear about this," Austin said.

"Yeah."

Austin turned him around and smiled. "Hungry?"

"I could eat," Jared said. "Morgan bought us lunch from Carl's, but don't worry. He went to get it."

"Good to know." Austin leaned down for a kiss. "Come on. There's a great steakhouse in Sevierville. I'm craving steak, and I can guarantee it's better than anything Carl can dish up."

* * *

Food ordered, Austin sat back in the booth and studied Jared for a moment. There was no easy way around the subject, so he just went for it. "Has your dad ever suspected your mother of cheating?"

Jared sighed and stared down into his Coke. "It wouldn't surprise me. She's always been entitled and flirted whenever she was around other men. But… Harlan Frost?" He grimaced. "Why?"

"Not something I personally want to contemplate," Austin said. He sipped his own Coke before continuing. "On a totally different topic, I'd love to see you pursue what you enjoy doing. The

University of Tennessee has an undergrad program in retail and hospitality management. It would be a good first step."

Jared looked up at him and chuckled. "You've really thought this out, haven't you?"

Austin shrugged. "I care about you, and I want to see you succeed." He reached out and grasped Jared's hand, giving it a gentle squeeze. "Let me help?"

"I'm not even sure where to start."

"That's easy to handle," Austin said. "We can sit down this weekend and get the ball rolling. What about Jamie? Has he ever expressed any interest in going to college?"

"Not really. He spent most of his life just trying to keep his head down and stay out of trouble, not that his dad and brother let him."

"Well, let's get you started down that road, and maybe he will find something he wants to do, too. Though, knowing Morgan, everything's already in progress."

Jared laughed. "I told y'all Jamie needs the discipline and structure." When he met Austin's gaze, there was a flash of heat in those deep brown eyes. "Speaking of discipline…"

Austin grinned and sat back when the server arrived with their food. Only when she left did he reply. He nodded toward Jared's plate and unwrapped his own silverware. "Eat, boy. I know where this topic is going. Yes, as I'd said before, I do give punishments when necessary. I'm assuming you want to know what they are."

Jared nodded and took a bite of steak.

"The primary method is orgasm denial," Austin said. He noted Jared's startled expression. "When we are having sex, in a full scene or not, I tell you not to come. That's only until I'm ready to allow you to do so. However, orgasm denial as punishment is far different. It has a set time, during which I will torment you, physically and not, while you would not be allowed to come. The shortest time would be a week."

Jared swallowed and blinked at him. "A… week?"

"Yes," Austin said. He took a bite of his own steak.

"You said the belt thing last night wasn't a punishment. Is it ever?"

"No. I use impact play because I thoroughly enjoy it, and, judging from your reactions, so do you."

Jared squirmed and stuffed a steak fry into his mouth. Austin just chuckled.

"Other punishments may involve chores you don't like doing, watching me pleasure myself with you unable to join in at all." He took a drink and smirked. "Then there's always a full cockcage."

"Uh…"

"Enclosed, with only a hole to piss out of," Austin explained. God, he loved watching the blush creep over Jared's skin. "Locked, of course."

Jared whimpered, and he dropped a hand under the table. One look from Austin, though, had the hand back on the tabletop. "Sir…"

"Now I want to know some things from you," Austin said. "What did you like about the restraints?"

Chapter Ten

Was 'everything' a good answer? Jared took a drink, a bite of steak, and thought about his reply. Austin didn't push him at all, just ate as well and waited patiently.

"I honestly don't know how to put it into words. At first, I thought 'everything,' but I'm guessing you want more than that."

"Good start," Austin said, "but, yes. It helps me to know what you did not like, what you liked, and what you *really* liked."

Jared chuckled. "Really liked, Sir?" He met Austin's gaze. "Knowing you could do anything you wanted to, and I couldn't move. I trust you, so there wasn't anything scary about it. I loved being at your mercy."

"Vulnerability can be a huge turn-on," Austin said. He finished his dinner and moved the plate to the side. "What about the belt?"

It took a good deal of self-control to not reach down and rub his hardening cock. Jared swallowed and moved his empty plate toward Austin's. He squirmed and swore he could still feel the belt slapping his ass.

"Yes, boy?"

"I loved it," Jared said, glancing back up at Austin. "I can, uh, understand why you like impact play."

Austin smirked. "Would you want to try other forms of it?"

"Like what? I mean, I know there are crops, floggers, whips, paddles, hands."

"Very good. I'm glad to know you've really done your research. I love the intimacy and personal aspect of using my hand or my belt. Barring those, I also enjoy paddles."

"Do you have a paddle?" It was miracle he got the question out. He clasped his hands on the tabletop to keep them there. God, he'd never been so fucking hard in his life, certainly not at the thought of a paddle, but he couldn't help it. Feeling Austin's belt on his ass had been insanely hot.

"I do," Austin said. "Do you want to see them?"

"Can we do more than look?" Jared asked with a grin he hoped came across as flirtatious. Judging by the way Austin gazed at him, it worked.

"We can indeed." Austin polished off his drink, and the server dropped off the check. He waited until she left again with his card before continuing. "Do you need to go home tonight?"

"I'm not sure Dad honestly expects me to come home on a regular basis," Jared said. "He seemed surprised to see me the last time. I'll send him a text, but… I'd love to stay with you if that's okay."

Smiling, Austin reached over and grasped Jared's hand. "It's more than okay. If it was up to me, you would be there all the time."

Jared blinked at him. "Really?"

"Yes. It's something we can discuss later. Tomorrow, we need to speak with Jamie, Morgan, Aida, and your dad. Tonight, however, I want nothing more than to introduce you to the pleasures of impact play beyond what we did."

"Yes, Sir," Jared murmured.

By the time they left the restaurant, it was dark outside. Austin put an arm around Jared's shoulders as they headed to the car. It felt better than Jared really had words for, to be honest. Austin was everything he'd always dreamed of in a lover: tall, strong, handsome, and with a firm knowledge of what it meant to be dominating and not domineering. The uniform, that Austin still wore, only added fuel to the fire.

"When we get home, I want you ready for me in the bedroom."

"Yes, Sir," Jared said. He slid into the passenger seat when Austin opened the door for him.

Austin got in as well, but before starting the car, he cupped the back of Jared's head and pulled him close. "I can't wait to see that sweet ass bright red."

Jared moaned into the kiss. Then Austin winked and started the car. Jared tucked his hands under his legs. It was going to be a long ride home.

* * *

Austin got the house locked up and headed for the bedroom. He didn't bother undressing since his boy loved the uniform. He stopped in the doorway and looked his fill.

Jared was such a wonderfully obedient and eager sub. He was on his knees beside the bed, nude and hard. He met Austin's gaze with hunger in those brown eyes. He watched as Austin went to the chest by the closet. Austin picked out one of his favorite

126

paddles and went to the bed. He sat down and patted his thigh.

"Over my knees, boy. Brace your hands on the floor."

Jared stood and draped himself over Austin's lap. Austin situated him so that Jared's hard cock rested between his thighs. Jared gasped softly when the material rubbed him.

"I'm going to start light," Austin said as he caressed the bare asscheeks that would soon be a beautiful shade of dark pink. "The paddle is wider than my hand, and the leather gives it a little more sting. There are also tiny rubber nubs that will add to the pain and pleasure. If you need to stop, what do you say?"

"Skillet, Sir," Jared murmured.

"Very good."

Austin picked up the paddle and lightly stroked it over Jared's ass. Jared squirmed a little, ass lifting upward. Austin tapped it with the paddle, just enough for Jared to feel the nubs.

Jared moaned. "Sir…"

The first light smack made Jared's breath catch. He gasped, body going rigid for the briefest moment. As soon as he seemed to relax a little, Austin gave his ass another pop with the paddle, a tiny bit harder. Jared whimpered softly.

"Ready, boy?"

"Yes, Sir," Jared said with a nod.

Austin gave him five swats in a row, the pressure behind each one hard enough to sting a bit, especially with the nubs. Jared panted and groaned, lean body trembling and rocking between Austin's thighs and the blows landing on his asscheeks.

Austin's own cock pressed against his pants, and every sound, every move from Jared only made it worse. By the time he stopped and set the paddle aside, he was more than ready to sink his cock in between those gorgeous red cheeks. He gave each one a hard squeeze, making Jared cry out.

"On the bed, on your knees, boy. I want that ass."

Jared stood on shaky legs with Austin's help, then crawled onto the bed. Head pillowed on his arms, he kept his ass in the air, legs spread. Austin knelt behind him and put on the rubber. Then he slicked two fingers.

"You should see your ass, boy," he said as he pushed both fingers into Jared's ass.

Jared moaned and pushed backward. "Sir…"

Austin couldn't wait any longer. He withdrew his fingers and sank his cock into tight heat. They both groaned, and Austin stilled for a few seconds once he was inside. Fingers digging into Jared's red cheeks, Austin set up a hard and fast rhythm. Jared cried out with every thrust inside. Austin squeezed Jared's cheeks a bit harder, then slapped the right one. Jared yelped and shoved back onto him.

"No coming," Austin growled as he took that sweet ass over and over. He shifted just enough to nail Jared's gland. "Fuck, yes…"

Entire body shaking, Jared panted and moaned, his pleas devolving into almost unintelligible sounds.

Austin smacked the other cheek hard and buried himself deep, grinding against Jared as he came.

Jared whimpered. "Oh, God... Sir..."

Austin pulled out and got rid of the rubber. Then he flipped Jared over, not missing the startled, desperate expression. Then he winked and bent down, taking Jared's cock into his mouth.

"Sir!" Hands grabbed Austin's hair, and Jared's hips snapped up. "Oh, fuck, fuck, please!"

Austin slid off long enough to say, "come," before swallowing him down again.

Jared shouted and filled Austin's mouth. Austin licked him clean and rose back up for a kiss. Jared didn't seem at all bothered when Austin passed the last bit of semen to him. Judging by the soft moan Jared fed him, Austin had the feeling his boy quite liked it.

"Did you like the paddle?"

Austin rose up and gently nudged Jared to roll over onto his stomach. Then he grabbed the aloe lotion from the bottle shelf of the bedside table. He began rubbing a small amount onto Jared's asscheeks. Jared practically melted into the mattress.

"It was perfect, Sir," Jared murmured. "So fucking perfect."

Chapter Eleven

"So… my dad is having an affair."

Jared blinked up at Jamie from across the bar. "Uh…"

"With your mom," Jamie added with a smirk.

"Yeah, we wanted to talk to you and Morgan," Jared said. "Also my dad and your mom."

Jamie sighed and leaned on the bar top, arms crossed. "Mom knows. She found some receipts my dad thought he hid. Dude, he's got a lot of money socked away. More than even she knew about."

"Good," Austin said as he joined them, Morgan right behind him. "If she pursues divorce, he is required, by law, to disclose *all* income and financial information."

"She is going to talk to a lawyer on Monday," Jamie said. "She's pissed. She confronted him, and he caved. Confessed the entire thing."

"As she is quite entitled to be," Morgan said. He grabbed two more Pepsi cans from the fridge for him and Austin. "While I honestly can't see what the hell Margie Haley sees in Harlan, I'm not the least bit surprised to know Harlan is having an affair. Aida doesn't deserve it, and that bastard certainly does *not* deserve Aida."

"What's your mom going to do in the meantime?" Jared asked.

Jamie snorted and took a sip of his drink. "She kicked him out, dude."

"Really?" Jared asked him with a grin.

"That's not all. When Daryl tried to argue with her and took Dad's side, Mom told him to leave, too."

Jared's jaw fell open.

Jamie laughed and nodded. "She said Daryl stormed out, shouting about how he's going to his girlfriend's where he's wanted."

"Wow…" Jared just shook his head.

"Whose name is on the trailer?" Austin asked.

"It's a rental," Jamie said. "Because her credit was better, Mom is the primary tenant listed. Hell, her income is what pays the bills anyway."

Austin nodded. "Good. If she needs help, she knows she can come to me. Harlan dropped by the other day, ranting about how our good doc here was corrupting 'his boy.' I made it very clear that you are an adult and this relationship has absolutely nothing to do with anyone but you and Morgan."

"Thanks," Jamie said. "I can't say I'm surprised he went to you."

"Dad said he wanted to talk to your mom, actually," Jared said. "You think she'll be okay with that?"

Jamie shrugged. "I don't see why not. Lemme text her."

As Jamie sent a text to his mother, Jared tilted his head up for a kiss. Austin's arm went around his shoulders, and Jared pressed a little closer.

"When Jamie is done, Morgan has an idea he wants to toss out."

Jared nodded and took another kiss. He could live off of Austin's kisses. "Yes, Sir."

Jamie laughed and set his phone on the bar, face up. "They beat us to the punch. They are in Sevierville, having lunch and discussing their pathetic, soon-to-be exes."

Jared leaned over and read the text aloud.

"Hi, baby. Actually, I reached out to Jack this morning. We are in Sevierville, having lunch and talking. He's such a sweet man, and he sure doesn't deserve that harpy."

Jared glanced up at Jamie. "Is it just me—"

"Nope," Jamie said with a laugh. "Not just you. I got the same impression."

"Make sure they both keep a lid on it—no matter what *it* is—until divorces are final," Austin said.

"Well, now that all the chaos has been addressed, I propose a long weekend," Morgan said. "Boys, get packed. I'm closing the office tomorrow, giving us a three-day weekend."

"What about you?" Jared asked, looking up at Austin.

"All taken care of," Austin said with a smile. "They know they can reach me on my cell, but only if it's an emergency."

"So where are we going?" Jamie asked Morgan.

"Nashville, boy," Morgan said. "Back to where it started."

Jamie jumped up and threw his arms around Morgan's neck, kissing the man. Jared laughed and relaxed against Austin's side.

"Let's head to your place and get your stuff for the weekend," Austin said, kissing the top of Jared's head.

Jared met Jamie's gaze once his best friend sat back down at the bar. Before Jared could even open his mouth, Jamie was talking.

"Sir," Jamie said to Austin, "it would be awesome if Jared could live closer."

Morgan popped Jamie on the ass and chuckled. "Brat."

Jamie looked completely unrepentant, but Jared wanted to sink into the floor.

"I agree," Austin said. He slipped a finger beneath Jared's chin and tilted his head up. "Thoughts, boy?"

Jared blinked up into those gorgeous blue eyes. "Yes, Sir," he murmured.

"Then it's settled." Austin kissed him softly. "We'll have a nice, long weekend in a hotel. Then we're moving you in when we get back."

Jared smiled. "I'd love that, Sir."

"So would I."

Jared looked back at Jamie and stuck his tongue out. "Ass, but thank you."

Shrugging, Jamie killed off the last of his drink. "If I don't say it, it'll never get said."

"Watch it, boy," Morgan growled.

Jamie blushed but managed to almost hide his smirk. "Sorry, Daddy."

* * *

Jared prayed his dad cleaned a little. He opened the front door and stepped side for Austin to walk in. Thankfully, the place wasn't a disaster.

"Will you be okay moving out and leaving your dad here alone?"

Jared smiled and led Austin toward his bedroom. "Yeah. He said he's surprised I haven't moved out yet. I think he's kind of looking forward to turning my room into an office, to be honest."

As Jared packed a bag for the weekend, he heard a car door. He glanced out the window. Then the front door opened.

"Hello?"

Jared went into the living room. Judging from the way his dad's eyes widened, Jared figured Austin was right behind him. "Hi, Dad."

"Um…" Dad blinked. "Everything okay?"

Austin chuckled and stepped around Jared, hand extended. "Good evening, Mr. Haley. Austin Russell."

Dad shook Austin's hand, gaze shifting between him and Jared. "Nice to meet you. I'm, well… you know who I am. I'm guessing everything's fine then."

"It is, Dad," Jared said.

Austin took his bag and surprised Jared with a light, chaste kiss. "I'll be outside." He nodded goodbye to Jared's dad and headed out.

"That's gonna take some getting used to," Dad muttered, staring out the front window. He turned to Jared. "The cop thing, I mean. As long as you're safe and happy, I don't care who you sleep with."

Jared hugged his dad. "Thanks, Dad."

Dad sighed and held him tight. "You don't have to thank me, Jared. You're my son, and I love you." He stepped back a little. "So when can I turn your bedroom into my office?"

Jared laughed and raked a hand through his hair. He slipped off his glasses and cleaned them on the hem of his shirt. "Um… this week." He put them back on and met his dad's gaze. "Will you be okay?"

Dad snorted. "Of course. Besides, I may not be… alone on occasion."

"So I heard," Jared said with a grin. "But Austin made a good point, too: don't let anyone know about you and Jamie's mom until after divorces are final."

"Oh, believe me, we won't," Dad said. "She's determined to rake Harlan through the mud and take everything she can get."

"Smart woman."

"And fiery," Dad added.

Jared tried to reconcile that idea with the Aida Frost he'd grown up knowing. It just didn't work. He shook his head. "No more, Dad. TMI."

Dad chuckled and gestured toward the front door. "Go on. I'm guessing you'll be gone all weekend?"

"Yeah, we, Morgan, and Jamie are going to Nashville. We'll be back Sunday night."

"Have fun, and whatever you do, do it safely."

Grinning, Jared opened the door and looked back at his dad. "Always, Dad. Always."

Chapter Twelve

Austin sat back in his chair, Morgan beside him, and watched Jared and Jamie dance. They ignored every other person on the dance floor, and, occasionally, one of them would glance over with a wink and a grin.

"Who would've thought a random encounter in a bar would've led to this?" Morgan said before taking a sip of beer.

Austin nodded, his own bottle nearly untouched. He'd been too busy watching a particularly lean body dancing most of the night. Thankfully, their hotel wasn't too far, so they'd all been able to walk over. Though, given what he—and most likely Morgan—had in mind, Austin had made it clear he and Jared would only have one drink each. Morgan had made the same rule for himself and Jamie.

One song merged into another, and Jamie and Jared were still going strong. The more Austin watched, the more his gaze kept straying to Jared's slender neck. He'd never collared anyone in the years he'd been in the lifestyle, but damned if the idea of seeing a thin leather collar with a lock around Jared's neck wouldn't leave his mind.

Morgan chuckled and finished his beer. "I know that look."

"It's too soon, I think."

"Maybe," Morgan said, "and maybe not. You know as well as I do that the only people with any say in it are you and Jared."

Austin couldn't argue with that logic. "Very true."

"Do you love him?"

He shot Morgan a 'what do you think' look. Morgan just smiled.

"Okay, point taken," Morgan said. "But does *he* know?"

"Not yet," Austin admitted. "I'm planning on telling him this weekend."

"Well, rest assured, that boy looks at you like you hung the moon. I don't doubt in the least that he feels the same way."

Austin hoped so. He took a drink just as Jared and Jamie returned to their table, both panting and sweaty. Jamie dropped onto Morgan's lap, arms draped over the man's shoulders, and kissed him. A few whistles came from various directions, and Morgan gave Jamie's ass a smack.

"I couldn't help it," Jamie said with a grin.

Morgan rolled his eyes, but his smile only widened. "I know the feeling, boy. You ready to head back to the hotel?"

Jamie nodded and gave Morgan another quick peck. "Yes, please, Daddy," he said, keeping his voice low.

Austin waved a hand at them while the other was wrapped around Jared's shoulders. Jared snuggled close, one hand on Austin's upper thigh. "Go on. We're gonna head out, too."

"We'll see you two in the morning," Morgan said as he and Jamie stood up. "Have fun."

Austin got up and pulled Jared with him. "Come on, boy. I'm thinking a nice, hot shower and payback for making me watch you grinding on Jamie are in order."

Jared laughed as they left the bar. Outside, he snaked an arm around Austin's waist on the way to the hotel down the block. "Sir…"

"Hmm?"

Jared stopped, as did Austin. "I need to say this. Now, not when we're in the middle of… things."

Austin smiled and pulled him close. "I'm listening."

Jared stared up at him. "It might seem too early, and maybe it is. I've never been in—"

Austin kissed him, silencing the babble. Jared's arms went around Austin's neck, and Jared moaned into the kiss.

"I love you, too," Austin whispered.

Jared nodded and pressed closer. "Yes," he murmured. "God, yes, Sir, I love you."

"Come on," Austin said, reluctantly pulling back a little. "I'm going to soap you down, then take advantage of you in every way I can think of."

"Please. I'll do anything, Sir."

Austin smirked and slapped Jared's ass hard, making his sub yelp. "I know, boy, and I'm going to remember that tonight when you're begging and pleading to come."

"Oh, God," Jared muttered.

Austin got them moving again. "Almost there. When we get into the room, I want you to get the shower going nice and hot. I'll join you once I get a few things."

By the time they reached the hotel, Austin was hard as steel. Judging from the quick glance at his sub's jeans, he figured Jared was just as eager. Austin unlocked the door with his keycard and held it open.

Jared rose up on tiptoes for a kiss and then went into the bathroom. Austin locked the door, set his phone, wallet, and card on the table beside Jared's glasses. Then he opened his suitcase. He heard the water going in the shower and the curtain drawing shut. Lube and cockring in hand, he went into the bathroom.

"I do love an obedient boy," he said as he undressed. He left the cockring on the counter.

Then he stepped into the shower and set the lube on a shelf before tugging Jared close. His sub moaned and rubbed against him, their cocks brushing along one another. Austin reached between them and gripped both in one hand.

"Oh, fuck," Jared groaned. He thrust into Austin's fist. "Sir, may I suck you?"

Austin released them and, hands on Jared's shoulders, gently push his boy to the tub floor. "I'm not ready to come, but I won't turn down feeling your mouth. Open up, boy."

Jared closed his eyes and hummed around Austin's cock. The vibrations traveled up Austin's shaft and into his balls. He held onto Jared's wet hair and pumped in and out, slow and easy.

"Fuck, your mouth is amazing," he murmured. When the pleasure was almost too much, he pulled back. "Let's get you nice and clean."

He helped Jared stand and began running soapy hands over Jared's body, head to toe. He kept his touches light as he washed Jared's cock and balls, and Jared whimpered. Austin chuckled and gestured for Jared to turn around. Then he repeated the washing. When he reached Jared's ass, he knelt and spread his sub's cheeks.

"Hold 'em, boy. Show me that pretty hole."

Jared reached back and held his cheeks open. He gasped when Austin leaned in for a lick. "Sir…"

Austin pressed his tongue into Jared and reached blindly for the lube. He kept up the licks and pushes inside while slicking up two fingers. Then he slid them inside and licked around them.

Jared moaned and rocked backward. Then Austin stood, thrusting his fingers in deep. "Sir!"

"Just making sure my boy is nice and ready," Austin whispered in Jared's ear. He scissored his fingers, making Jared moan again. Then he withdrew them. "Time to get out. I have something for you."

Water off, Austin stepped out first. He picked up the cockring and grinned. Jared dried off, though his gaze never left the thin leather strip. Austin sat on the toilet lid and pulled Jared to stand between his legs.

"You will not come until told to do so," Austin said as he gave Jared's hard cock a slow stroke. He snapped the cockring around the base and flicked the

head with his tongue. Jared gasped, hips jerking. "Bed,
boy. You're going to ride me tonight."

After Austin grabbed the lube, they went into
the main room, and Austin stretched out on his back.
He stroked his cock slowly, entranced by the way Jared
crawled over him.

Austin held up the lube and a rubber. "Give me
a good show."

Biting one corner of his lower lip, Jared slicked
up two fingers and turned so Austin could see those
fingers sink into Jared's ass. Jared moaned as he
worked his own hole, and Austin had to grip the base
of his cock to stave off coming right then and there the
second he got the rubber on it.

"Now, boy."

Jared twisted back around and straddled
Austin. Then Austin groaned as he sank into tight,
slick heat. Hands on Jared's hips, he guided his boy up
and down, rocking his hips, grinding into Jared's ass
with every thrust inside.

Hands braced on Austin's chest, Jared stared
down at him, eyes wide, mouth open. If Austin hadn't
already fallen, the vision above him would've done it.
Jared's hard cock leaked precome, and Jared shivered.
Knowing how close he was, Austin anchored his feet
on the bed and slammed into him.

"Now," he growled as he unsnapped the
cockring. "Come on my cock."

Jared threw his head back and shouted. Come
spurted onto Austin's belly, and Jared's ass clamped
tight around him. Austin grunted and pinned Jared
down onto his cock as he came.

Panting, Jared collapsed onto Austin's chest, apparently not caring about the mess. He kissed Austin's neck. "You're perfect, Sir. Love you."

Austin smiled and stroked one hand up and down his lover's spine. "Love you, too, Jared. Very much."

ABOUT THE AUTHOR

Mychael Black has been writing professionally since 2005. He writes gay romance and erotica, but also het romance as Carys Seraphine and queer fantasy as Katherine Cook.

He's an avid PC gamer with a love for RPGs, a horror fanatic, and a fantasy nut. He also has a weakness for anything relating to skulls, dogs, and Spongebob Squarepants.

Mychael lives on the Eastern Shore of the US with his family. He loves to hear from readers, be it via email or Facebook.

https://www.mychaelblack.com

https://www.facebook.com/mblackauthor/